JOAN HIATT HARLOW

STAR

in the

STORM

SCHOLASTIC INC.

New York Toronto London Auckland Sydney
Mexico City New Delhi Hong Kong Buenos Aires

ISBN-13: 978-0-439-89992-5
ISBN-10: 0-439-89992-3

12 11 10 9 8 7 6 5   8 9 10 11/0

Printed in the U.S.A.   40

First Scholastic printing, November 2006

Designed by Michael Nelson

Map by Kristan J. Harlow Delphia

The text for this book was set in Lomba Book.

In loving memory of my mother,
Maggie Wells Small Hiatt, R.N., a Newfoundlander
who sang me the songs and told me the tales.

J. H. H.

CONTENTS

*

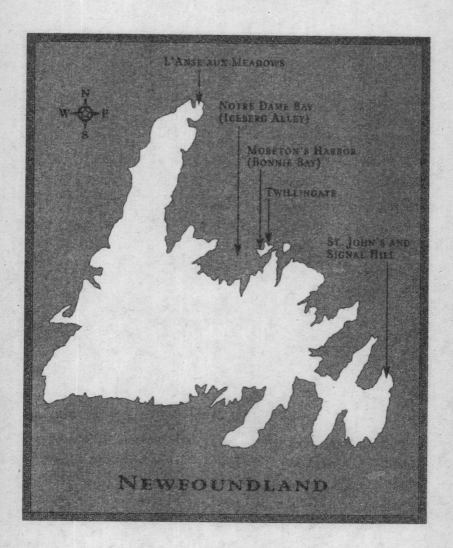

L'Anse aux Meadows

Notre Dame Bay
(Iceberg Alley)

Moreton's Harbor
(Bonnie Bay)

Twillingate

St. John's and
Signal Hill

N
W · E
S

NEWFOUNDLAND

ELEVEN BLACK BIRDS

A FLOCK OF HUGE BLACK BIRDS SOARED, GATHERED, then landed one after another in the trees near Maggie. She paused in her walk up the hill, blocked her eyes against the spring sun, and counted.

"'One for sadness, two for mirth,'" Maggie quoted the old rhyme about crows and ravens her mother had taught her. "'Three for marriage, four for birth; five for laughing, six for crying; seven for sickness, eight for dying; nine for silver, ten for gold; eleven for a secret that will never be told.'

"A secret," she whispered to the black Newfoundland dog by her side. She smiled as she thought of her father's warnings about *pishogues* —superstitious foolishness. "Everyone in Bonnie Bay has a secret, I'll wager."

The cliff behind Maggie's house rose sharply. At the top it took on the shape of a face peering down into the harbor. Everyone in the little fishing outport called the cliff the *quidnunc*. Like a *quidnunc*, or busybody, the rock jutted its chin over the tops of the trees as if straining to see the folk of Bonnie Bay in the British Colony of Newfoundland.

Maggie Wells and her dog, Sirius, were climbing to the top of the *quidnunc*. Sirius lingered for a moment on Witch's Rock, a ledge on the hillside that overlooked the harbor.

"C'mon, Sirius," Maggie coaxed. "I know you'd love to plunge right into the ocean, but that water is too cold. And now there's a big iceberg in the harbor."

Sirius turned and trudged behind Maggie as she headed up the steep path. From the time he was a pup, Sirius had loved swimming and diving from the wharves along the waterfront. He was always happy to fetch things from the boat for Pa, or to work around the stages—the long wharves of rough-hewn tree limbs where freshly caught fish were laid out to dry.

When they reached the top of the *quidnunc*, Maggie sat on the edge of the smooth-faced rock and carefully slid down to a wide, rocky ledge that was carpeted with soft moss. Sirius followed her cautiously. A thicket of sweet-smelling spruce concealed a small cave in the rocks. Sirius waited outside while Maggie crawled into the cave. She found an old baby blanket she had hidden there last fall and some shards of dishes she had used last year for a make-believe kitchen. The blanket was damp and musty, so she brought it out and hung it on a limb to air. I suppose twelve is too old to play copy house, Maggie thought. She set the dishes on a rock next to where Sirius was lying in the sun. "It's kind of sad to grow up, though," she whispered as she scratched her dog's ears.

Suddenly, an unripe berry plopped on her shoulder. Then another berry caught in her long brown braid.

"I know you're there, Vera," Maggie called, looking around.

A curly, blond head poked out from behind a rock on the ledge above. "I followed you and Sirius all the way up here, and you never even saw me." Vera made her way down to Maggie. Her impish grin hardly matched the prim dress and starched white pinafore she wore. It always amazed Maggie that anyone as mischievous as her cousin, Vera, could stay so spotless and neat.

"It's neither ladylike nor Christian to spy on people." Maggie often pretended to scold her cousin as if she were several years younger instead of only a year. "Have you seen the iceberg off Killock Rock Island? It looks just like a church with two steeples."

Vera scrambled back up to the top of the *quidnunc* and looked to the north, where the iceberg towered high above the cliffs, blocking the narrows where Bonnie Bay opened into the sea.

"It's like a fairy castle," Vera whispered, "with turrets and towers."

"No, it's a church," insisted Maggie, climbing up after Vera. "I wonder if the iceberg that sank the *Titanic* was as big as that."

"Probably bigger," said Vera. It had only been a couple of months since the sinking of the famous ocean liner off the coast of Newfoundland. It was the biggest news during the spring of 1912, and the girls couldn't stop thinking about the tragedy.

"I'll *never* go near an iceberg," said Maggie. "It's way too dangerous."

"Look down there on Witch's Rock." Vera pointed. "There's Tamar Rand looking exactly like a witch herself, with her hair all mops and brooms."

"Can she see us?"

"She's looking back at the meadow. I think she's watching her sheep." Vera backed away slightly as if to hide herself from the girl below.

"Oh, Lord," whispered Maggie. "I don't want her to see us when we go back, especially when we have Sirius with us. You know how the Rands hate dogs. Pa says they're trying to make a law that will ban dogs from this whole bay."

"What will you do with Sirius if the law is passed?" asked Vera.

"Pa says we'll have to send him off somewhere, but I have something planned, all right," said Maggie, nodding. "I won't let them take Sirius away from me."

Sirius, who had been dozing on the soft bed of spruce needles, looked up and wagged his tail.

Maggie wound her long braid until it sat like a knot on the top of her head, then let it tumble back down to her waist. She peered below to Witch's Rock. Tamar stood looking out at the sea, her long dress fluttering around her ankles.

"When we go back, we'll walk right by her," said Vera, drawing herself up tall. "Those Rands do not own the *quidnunc.*"

"But they do own most everything else around here," Maggie said. "Our dads fish for old Howard, so it would be best not to cause any trouble."

Howard Rand was the richest man in Bonnie Bay. He had a large herd of sheep, and owned more boats than any of his neighbors. Maggie's father and Vera's father, Maggie's Uncle Norm, worked as fishermen on one of Howard Rand's boats. It was the custom for the owner of a boat to divide the catch of fish with his men. Then the owner would take back some fish from each shareman to help pay toward the costs of running the boat. But old Rand was known to charge unfair costs to his men. That and his sour disposition made him the most disagreeable skipper in Bonnie Bay. However, he had the best boats and fishing gear, and most folks considered it a privilege to work for him.

Maggie climbed back down to the mossy ledge, with Vera and Sirius close behind. She folded her blanket, gathered her china, and crawled into the little cave. Maggie thought about the eleven black birds. *A secret that'll never be told.* "Remember, you must *never, never* tell anyone about this cave," she warned Vera, who had followed her inside. "This is our secret. Do you swear?"

Vera held up her right hand. "I swear," she said solemnly.

Maggie hid her blanket and dishes on a stone ledge inside the cave. Then the girls climbed up to the top of the *quidnunc* and onto the path that took them back to the village. Sirius lumbered along ahead of them, wagging his silky tail.

When they approached Witch's Rock, the girls were frightened by the sound of growling, snarling dogs. Sirius began to bark. Suddenly, a sheep darted out from the bushes, bolting toward the cliff where Tamar was standing. She turned and shrieked as two vicious dogs came after the sheep. The sheep lost its footing on the rocky soil and plummeted off the boulder into the churning water below.

Screaming, Maggie and Vera raced to the edge and looked down. Maggie could see the sheep floating in the water.

"Your dog frightened it!" screamed Tamar, her dark eyes blazing as the two strange dogs bounded out of sight.

Before Maggie could answer, Sirius ran to the edge of the cliff and pawed the air, first with one paw and then the other. Suddenly, he sprang off the rock and down into the sea.

"He'll be killed!" Maggie howled. She peered fearfully over the cliff edge. Sirius's big head was bobbing up and down as he swam toward the sheep. Grabbing hold of the sheep's fleece with his teeth, the dog dragged his heavy burden back to the shore.

"He saved the sheep," Vera said excitedly. "He dove from the cliff to save the sheep."

Tamar scrambled down the path to the beach. "If I had a gun, I'd shoot that dog."

Maggie and Vera followed her to where Sirius was sniffing the lifeless animal.

"It's dead!" Tamar said accusingly. She waggled a finger at Maggie. "You and that dog will pay for this, you can be sure."

"We don't even know those dogs that attacked your sheep," Maggie protested. "My dog tried to save it. He dove all that way into the water to bring it back."

"My poor little sheep. She was about to yean, and I would have had a little lamb." Tears streamed down Tamar's cheeks. "You'll be sorry!" Tamar shook her fist at Maggie and narrowed her eyes. Her sharp features made Maggie think of a witch. "I'll see to it something terrible happens to all of you!"

"That's a right awful thing to say, Tamar!" Maggie snapped. "You know perfectly well that Sirius is a good dog."

"I'm going back and tell my Pa," said Tamar. She ran up the path toward town.

"C'mon," said Maggie as she headed for the road. "Let's go home."

Sirius sniffed at the sheep again. His tail wagged slowly, then he turned and followed Vera.

"That Tamar is a terrible witch," said Maggie angrily, "unjustly accusing Sirius."

"I wonder what she's going to do?" Vera shuddered. "She scares me."

"Pa will take care of it," Maggie said confidently.

"He'll make it right with old Howard Rand."

Pa and Ma Wells were at the kitchen table having four o'clock tea when Maggie stomped in breathlessly, Vera and Sirius at her heels.

"Ma! Pa!" she hollered without stopping to take off her shoes. "We're in a lot of trouble. Listen to what just happened."

Vera sat on the floor by the door and unbuttoned her black boots. "That witch, Tamar!" she spit out bitterly. "She's cursed us."

After Maggie and Vera had told their story, Pa asked, "Whose dogs chased the sheep?"

"I don't know," said Maggie. "One was black and the other was spotted. They're not Newfoundlands, like Sirius."

"Maybe they come from Whale's Gulch," Vera said.

"What will old Rand do?" Maggie grabbed her father's arm anxiously. "Will he shoot Sirius?"

"Of course not!" Ma burst out, her red-haired temper flaring.

"Probably the worst that will happen is that Rand will try to charge us the price of the sheep from my share of the fish," said Pa.

"At any rate, you can never tell till after," said Ma. "Try not to worry." She stroked Maggie's head and turned to Vera, who was still on the floor, leaning against Sirius. Ma shook her head. "Vera, don't sit there on the floor, maid. You'll get a draft. You don't look well. Are you all right?"

"I'm all right, Aunt Grace," said Vera, getting to her feet, "except I have a little headache."

"How long have you had a headache?" Ma felt Vera's head. "You're feverish, Vera. You should go home to bed."

"Probably all the excitement," said Pa with a wink at Vera. "That Tamar is enough to give anyone a headache."

"She cursed us." Vera shivered. "Just like a witch. She pointed her finger and said we'd be sorry." Suddenly, her face paled as she looked at something through the window.

Sirius stood up attentively, his head cocked.

Coming through the gate was Howard Rand, his ruddy face flushed with anger. Tamar was running behind him. "You shoot that dog, Papa. You show them they can't kill our sheep."

Maggie gasped. Old Rand was carrying a rifle!

ANGRY ENCOUNTER

P<small>A STRAIGHTENED HIMSELF TO HIS FULL SIX FEET,</small> then opened the door.

Howard Rand stood on the porch with Tamar at his side. "I've come to shoot your dogs," he said, brandishing his rifle.

"Oh, have you?" Pa's voice was calm.

Vera clung to her aunt. Maggie turned and quietly led Sirius out the back door and across the rock garden to her great-uncle Jabe Taylor's big white house. "Please hide Sirius for me," she begged the elderly man who was working in the garden.

"Hide that huge lout of a dog?" Uncle Jabe laughed. "That's not an easy thing to do, maid."

"Howard Rand is going to shoot him," Maggie explained. "Please, Uncle Jabe."

Without another word, the old man led the

unresisting dog into the house. Maggie could hear Aunt Gertrude's shrill voice. "Don't bring that dirty animal in here!"

"Hush your mouth, woman," Jabe retorted as he closed the door. Maggie raced back to her own house, hoping the Rands hadn't seen her lead Sirius away.

The Rands were still at the door. "I only have one dog," Pa was saying. "The one who tried to rescue your sheep."

"Rescue!" snorted old Rand. "Chased her right off the cliff, you mean."

"Is that the story Tamar told you?" Pa asked.

"It's true." Tamar tossed her long hair.

"I understand there were other dogs . . ." began Pa. "A spotted one . . ."

"Sirius has a spot on his chest. Besides, one dog or two—what does it matter?" Tamar interrupted shrilly. "My sheep was about to yean, and now she and her lamb are both dead. You are the only people around here with a black dog."

"The dogs probably came from across the bay," continued Pa, his voice cool and even. "Tamar will tell you my dog tried to save that sheep."

"Our dog is gentle," said Ma angrily. "He has

never hurt a sheep, and there are enough of them wandering loose everywhere."

Pa started to close the door. "We'll not be crosscacklin' with you anymore. Don't come to my home with threats and a gun or I'll have the constable after *you*."

"There's a law being passed, you know," Rand called out as Pa shut the door, "and when it is, I'll see that dog of yours is put down."

Maggie watched through the window as Tamar and her father walked over the hill and out of sight.

"Howard Rand is a big bluff," snorted her father. "He knows Sirius never harmed any sheep." He touched Maggie's arm. "But we'd better keep Sirius close to home, Maggie, just in case."

Ma slumped into a chair. "What would we do without Sirius?" she asked, shaking her head. "He hauls our firewood across the bay in the winter and helps around the stages in the summer. Why, he's a blessing to everyone in Bonnie Bay."

"Well, I know what *I'll* do if that law really does go through," said Maggie with a toss of her braid. "They'll just have to find Sirius first before they take him away from me!"

Vera's eyes brightened for a moment. "Oh, I know what you'll do, Maggie," she said. "You'll—"

"Hush, Vera," warned Maggie with a harsh glance.

"Hiding Sirius is about the same as trying to hide a schooner in a berry patch," laughed Uncle Jabe, who suddenly appeared in the doorway with Sirius by his side. "I made him lie under our kitchen table," he said. "A leg out at every corner. Not to mention that waggin' tail!"

"No, it wouldn't be easy to hide a big dog like Sirius," agreed Pa.

Ma began to clear the table. "Maggie, would you and Vera run down to Art's store and pick up some tea for me?"

"Not me," said Vera, rubbing her forehead. "My head's pounding like a drum. I think I'll go home."

"Off you go," said Ma, casting an anxious look at Pa. "You look right feverish, maid. Get yourself home and tell your mother I'll be over later."

Vera stood up, a bit wobbly. Her face was puffy and pink with fever. "Bye, Maggie." She picked up her boots and went outside in her stocking feet.

As Vera headed for her own house, Maggie went the other way, down the stony dirt road to Art's store, which stood next to the stages on the waterfront. Art had the only wireless telegraph equipment on this part of the island. Fishermen from the bay often gathered there to hear the weather, as well as the fishing and shipping news, which was sent by code.

Inside Art's, several fishermen stood talking around a slim boy.

"Once we put a little weight on him and fatten him up, he'll be fit enough," said Otto Hosmer, who had his arm about the boy's shoulders.

"As long as ye don't work him to death," laughed toothless Marcus Kelly.

Uncle Jabe stepped into the store and joined the group. "After where he lived in the Labrador, this place is a bustling city. He'll find plenty to keep him busy here." He gave the gaunt boy a hearty whack on the back.

The boy caught sight of Maggie and turned away.

"Come in, maid," said Art in a booming voice. "Come here and meet our new boy. He'll be living with Otto. His name's Cliff Bowen. Cliff, this here's

Maggie Wells. She lives up the hill in the yellow house. Her pa and his brother, Norm, are two of Rand's sharemen."

"Hullo," said Cliff, looking down at his feet.

"Hello," said Maggie. The boy seemed to be a few years older than she was.

"Cliff left his home way up in the Labrador, to live here in Bonnie Bay with us," Otto explained. "He's a bright boy, and we're hoping he can go to a university once he takes his tests."

Maggie knew that fishermen who traveled up the northern peninsula and into Labrador sometimes brought home children from poor families. They would have a better life, in exchange for help with the chores. Maggie had heard that Otto's brother had recently traveled to Labrador and brought a boy back. So this must be him, she thought.

"Maggie's the girl who owns the huge dog you were fancying," said Otto.

"His name is Sirius," said Maggie.

"Whar'd you get a name like that?" asked Cliff.

"It's after the brightest star in the sky, in the constellation of Sirius, the Great Dog. He has a white star on his black chest, so 'Sirius' seemed right," Maggie explained. "You can come up and see him sometime, if you like."

"If old Rand doesn't shoot the dog first," warned Marcus.

"Rand was in here after talking to your pa," Art said to Maggie. "He's getting together a group of sheep owners from other bays to put some pressure on about passing the dog law."

"Sheepherding dogs won't be bothered by the law," said Otto. "Why don't you teach Sirius to herd sheep?"

"There's an idea!" agreed Art.

"We don't have sheep," Maggie answered. "May I have some tea, please?"

"What's that scratching noise?" asked Art as he poured tea into a paper bag.

A bark came from outside. Cliff opened the door, and there stood Sirius, his tail flapping. In his collar was a piece of paper. Maggie took it and read, "'Please bring home two pounds of salt pork.'"

"What a dog," laughed Art, cutting off a slab of pork. "Knows right where to come with his message."

Sirius barked again and came inside, pushing past Maggie and Cliff.

"Now you can meet my dog properly," Maggie said to Cliff. "This is Sirius."

Sirius sat down and held out his large paw to Cliff, who shook it gently. Then, the dog sniffed at Cliff and drooled on the boy's boots.

"You're so lean, if he jumped on you he'd knock you over in a second," said Marcus, flashing another toothless grin. Maggie couldn't remember ever seeing Marcus with teeth. They had been knocked out in a brawl years ago.

"This is a good dog to take fishing." Otto scratched Sirius's ears. "Maggie's pa, Reuben, keeps him at the gunwale ready to grasp the fish should they slip off the hook."

"And if one does," added Art as he wrapped the pork in brown paper, "Sirius dives under the water and retrieves it."

Cliff shook his head in disbelief.

Maggie nodded vigorously. "It's true," she said. "And when Pa goes duck hunting, Sirius will leap into the roughest water, find the duck, and bring him back to Pa without loosing a feather."

"There's many a story we can tell you about this dog," said Uncle Jabe. "It'll be a loss to Bonnie Bay if anything happens to Sirius."

"The problem is that sheep *are* being destroyed by packs of dogs in many of the outports. So consequently many innocent dogs and families will have to suffer," said Otto. "Old Rand is taking up the cry here in Bonnie Bay. Folks are fighting to get the law passed in other places, too."

Marcus spoke up. "There are two sides to every coin."

Maggie's face flushed in anger. "That Tamar lied when she said Sirius chased her sheep off the cliff. She'd lie in court, too."

"Now that's a right serious thing you're saying, Maggie," said Otto. "Better find a legal way to keep Sirius. Calling names never helped any cause."

Maggie didn't respond. Taking her package, she led Sirius to the door. "Come see Sirius whenever you want," she said to Cliff.

"Thanks!" Cliff replied with a nod.

Maggie and Sirius walked to their square yellow house on the rocky hillside. To offset the gray of the rock cliffs, people in Bonnie Bay painted their homes in combinations of yellows, reds, blues, and whites. The houses faced every direction. Sometimes one house fronted another's back door, and sometimes only a tiny path led from one house to the next. Rickety fences marked property lines and gardens where potatoes, carrots, and turnips grew. In summer, flowers splashed the village with color. Now, in early June, a few patches of snow remained in the shaded spots in the woodlands, and flowers were not yet in bloom. The brightest colors in Bonnie Bay were the houses themselves. The hillside overlooking the water looked like a colorful quilt.

Vera's house was bright blue and stood just across the stony path from Maggie's yellow one. As Maggie approached, she noticed unusual activity. Ma and Pa were running up the steps into Vera's house.

Lucy Kelly, Marcus's wife, was heading from her small green house over to Vera's. She was frequently called upon to help out when someone was very ill. To see Lucy Kelly heading for Vera's was a bad sign for sure.

Maggie remembered Vera's headache. Had something awful happened to her cousin? Maggie began to run.

SICKNESS

VERA *COULDN'T* BE SICK. HADN'T SHE CLIMBED ALL the way up the *quidnunc* today?

Maggie and Sirus hurried up the steps to Vera's porch. "Wait here," she told the dog.

In the parlor, Vera's parents, Uncle Norm and Aunt Selina, knelt by the sofa where Lucy was bending over Vera's still form. Ma and Pa stood by helplessly.

"Maybe she's only fainted," said Ma consolingly.

"She's burning up with fever," Lucy said, rubbing Vera's hands.

"She was unconscious for several minutes before we called you," cried Aunt Selina, panic in her voice.

"I'll go to Twillingate and get Dr. Auld," said Pa. "I'll hitch up the horse right now."

Aunt Selina clutched her husband's arm. "It would be faster if you took the boat."

"The iceberg is blocking the harbor," said Uncle Norm. "We can't get through."

"I'll go by wagon." Pa rushed by Maggie.

"What can I do?" asked Maggie.

"Go home, Maggie," said Ma gently. "You can trim the lamps and start the potatoes for supper."

"But I want to stay here with Vera," Maggie protested.

"No, go along home, dear."

Reluctantly, Maggie stepped out onto the porch. Sirius lifted his head and thumped his tail.

"Come on, dog," Maggie said sadly. "We're not needed here." They walked back home, where Pa was hitching up the horse and wagon.

"Will Vera die?" Maggie asked her father.

"Try not to worry, maid," said Pa, swinging himself up on the seat. "I'm going for help now. You take care of things around here." The wagon clattered down the hill, out of sight.

Maggie went into the house, dropped her parcel onto the kitchen dresser, and lined up the lanterns. After pulling a pail from behind the door, she went outside to the well, which the Wellses shared with three other families—Uncle Norm's, Uncle Jabe's, and Otto's. While Sirius stood by, Maggie walked carefully around the broken boards that served as a cover for the top of the well and pumped until the pail was full of water.

She carried the heavy bucket back to the house, set a pan of water on the stove, and opened the damper. The wood fire began to crackle and flame, and Sirius stretched out close to the warm stove.

Taking a sharp knife, Maggie trimmed away the hard crust that lined the top of the lantern wicks.

Maggie looked anxiously out the window. There was no sign of anyone. Finally she ran outside to Vera's.

Sirius, who had jumped up to follow, yelped softly as the door swung back on him. He pawed the door until it opened and trotted after his mistress.

"Ma!" Maggie called quietly. "Ma!"

Ma appeared in the doorway. "There's no change, Maggie," she said. She hugged Maggie and kissed her hair. "Go home and pray, maid."

She went back into the house, closing the door softly behind her.

Maggie sat down on the steps and buried her head in her hands. "Lord and Father," she whispered, "please be with thy servant Vera. She's my only cousin and she's such fun. Surely Thou must have some useful plan for her life. Help her to be well, please . . . please . . ." Maggie felt a nudge at her elbow. Sirius poked his huge silky head under Maggie's arm and started to lick her face. Maggie threw her arms around the dog's neck and wept. "I love you, my good dog," she said. Sirius moved closer, burrowing his nose in her neck.

"Stop, Sirius! Stop tickling me!" She wiped her face with her sleeve and smiled. "You slobbery old thing!" Sirius backed away, and Maggie hugged him again. "Good star dog," she said.

Maggie thought of Tamar standing on Witch's Rock, her black dress flapping around her ankles, and how she had threatened Sirius. Now Vera was lying unconscious. Did Tamar Rand truly have some dark and terrible power?

* * *

Maggie fell into a fitful sleep that night. Once, she awakened and could see there were lights still shining over at Vera's house. The waning moon was rising over the *quidnunc*, and Maggie wondered which was closer, the moon or Heaven.

Ma peeked into Maggie's room. "How is Vera?" asked Maggie.

"She's in a coma." Ma's voice was somber. "We're still waiting on Pa and the doctor."

"Tamar cursed us!" Maggie exclaimed. "I didn't believe she could, but look what's happening to Vera."

"Oh, balderdash!" Ma looked tired. There were dark circles under her eyes. Her red hair was pulled back in a tight bun, and her face was pale in the moonlight. "Just where do you think Tamar suddenly acquired this power?"

"I don't know, but I've been praying really hard, and Vera still isn't better."

"'A day is with the Lord as a thousand years,'" quoted Ma. She sat on Maggie's bed and took her hand. "Time is different for Him. As for us . . . well, we have to be patient, even though it's hard sometimes."

"I wish I could do something to help Vera." Maggie leaned back as her mother pulled the blankets over her.

"We'll see in the morning." Ma kissed Maggie and left the room.

Moonlight crept between the limbs of the crab apple tree and made dancing shadows on Maggie's wall.

There was no change in Vera's condition the next morning. Ma was next door, keeping watch with Vera's mother. Maggie raced across the stone walk in her nightgown to see what was happening. Sirius was on the porch chewing on a ham bone. He looked up briefly and wagged his tail.

Vera, now in her own bed upstairs, was still flushed with fever.

"It's me, Vera," whispered Maggie. "Please speak to me. Please?"

Vera didn't move.

"Get ready for church now, Maggie," Ma said. "Vera needs all the prayers she can get."

Sirius followed Maggie back into her house.

Upstairs in her room, Maggie unbraided her hair. Does God hear prayers better when they're said at church? she wondered as she combed her hair with her mother's big ivory comb. She put on her blue dress with the white piping around the collar.

Maggie went to the desk in the parlor, pulled out a small box, and opened it. Nestled on the black velvet interior was a silver brooch with amber and topaz stones that glistened in the light from the window. Maggie ran her finger over the rough surface. The Celtic brooch was the family's only treasure. The pin had been handed down from generation to generation for so long, no one could remember its exact origin.

Maggie knew there was a magic about that pin. Perhaps it belonged to a knight—after all, it had a crest on it, and something written in Latin, Ma said. Maggie thought about her forebears who had worn and cared for the brooch so that it still glistened and sparkled even after hundreds of years. Perhaps if she wore the brooch today—for Vera—it would bring good luck. Maggie frowned. Superstitious foolishness, she thought. *Pishogues!*

Sirius entered the parlor, wagging his silken tail.

"Naughty boy," Maggie said sternly. "You know you're not allowed in the parlor."

Sirius nudged Maggie's hand. She held the box with the pin under his nose. "See the precious stones? This brooch is our family heirloom." Sirius sniffed curiously, and Maggie pulled the box away. "And it would be best if you didn't drool all over it!" Sirius sat and thumped his tail on the wooden floor.

Would it hurt to wear the brooch today? After all, it was hers—at least someday it would be her very own. Yes, she would wear it to church. She fastened the heavy, ornate brooch to her neckline.

Ma came home long enough to braid Maggie's hair and fix her some biscuits and partridgeberry jam for breakfast. Before heading back to Vera's house, Ma noticed the brooch on Maggie's dress. She hugged her daughter. "It's all right, my child," she said. "Wear it today."

The stove fire had died, and Maggie poured herself a cup of switchel—yesterday's tea, now cold and strong. Before heading down the hill to the white church in the village, Maggie called to Sirius. "C'mon," she said. "They'll never shoot you at church, or on Sunday."

Sirius barked and pranced around Maggie happily as they strolled down the road together. They met Cliff and Otto, who were also headed to church. Maggie noticed how smart Cliff looked in his new clothes.

"How's Vera?" asked Otto.

"No better." Maggie sighed. "We're still waiting on Dr. Auld."

"We'll say a prayer for her this morning," Otto said.

Cliff patted Sirius, who licked his hand. Then he waved and walked on ahead with Otto.

Sirius stayed close to Maggie. As she rounded the bend she saw Lucy Kelly and her daughter, Annie, entering the church. Annie had on the dress she wore every Sunday. The Kellys were probably the poorest family in Bonnie Bay. Lucy Kelly often took on small jobs around the village, and folks paid her with food or clothes, or sometimes some small amounts of money. She looked worn and older than her years. Many times Maggie heard her mother say, "Poor Lucy. Her husband, Marcus, is never around to help her." Maggie had known Annie all her life, and she felt a sudden surge of sadness for both Annie and her mother.

Sirius lay down on the front lawn while Maggie went inside the church. The singing had started, and Maggie stood in her family's empty pew. She loved the hymn singing best of all and joined in before she had even opened her hymnbook.

"'Jesus, Savior, pilot me, over life's tempestuous sea . . .'"

When the song and prayer ended, Maggie settled down to hear the sermon. At first she listened carefully to hear if the Reverend Dobbs said anything that would explain what happened to Vera, but the pastor spoke only about being a good neighbor and not bearing false witness or telling lies about one's friends.

Maggie's eyes began to roam. Sitting up front were the Rands. Tamar sat up straight, looking neither to the left nor right, her hands folded in her lap. Her father and mother sat rigidly on either side of her. Tamar was the only child left at home now that her sister, Marie, had married and moved away to the city of St. John's.

Maggie scowled. How could Tamar sit there and listen to a sermon about being a good neighbor when she herself had lied about Sirius and swore something terrible would happen to Maggie and Vera?

Maggie stood up suddenly and strode to the back of the church. Several people stared. Tamar turned and looked at Maggie with narrowed eyes.

Maggie walked into the sunlight. Sirius lumbered over to meet her. "C'mon, Sirius," she said. "This is no place for us, with Tamar Rand sitting in there in the front pew all pious and Christian. A lot of good it does for her to learn about bearing false witness, when she lies about you."

So Maggie and her dog went back around the harbor road, by the cemetery, and up the hill. A flock of ravens circled overhead, and Maggie counted them. Seven. *Seven for sickness, eight for dying.* She counted them again. *There must not be eight.*

"*Seven,*" she whispered in relief. "Sickness— but *not* dying."

At Vera's house, Maggie tiptoed through the

open door. Sirius headed for his own porch.

Maggie's mother and aunt were at the kitchen table, drinking tea. Both of them looked tired.

"I thought you were at church," Ma said.

"I left early," said Maggie. "The sermon was so boring, I almost fell asleep."

Ma smiled, and even Aunt Selina seemed to brighten for a moment. "That pastor was sent to Bonnie Bay because no one else wanted him, I'm sure," Aunt Selina said.

"But it wasn't polite to walk out, Maggie," her mother admonished.

"How is Vera?" Maggie asked.

"Ah, there's a true scrimshank if I ever heard one," said Ma, grabbing Maggie's hand and pulling her close. She hugged her, then held her out at arm's length, pretending to scold. "Trying to change the subject, eh? Well, walking out on the reverend will get you in trouble with the Lord."

Maggie crossed her arms. "Even the Lord would have been bored with Reverend Dobbs's sermon." She paused. "Ma, does God hear prayers in churches more than He hears prayers outside of churches?"

"I'm sure He hears prayers wherever they are offered."

"I'm going up to see Vera." Maggie headed for the stairs. "Oh, I saw seven ravens today, Ma. That means sickness."

"Most people think they're just crows," said Aunt Selina. "Big crows."

"Hmm," Maggie said. "Oh, well, it doesn't matter. My friends at school say the same verse for crows, only they cross themselves whenever they see one."

"Crows or ravens, it's just superstition," Ma said. "With all those big black birds around here, your friends would be crossing themselves all day long. Speaking of school, Maggie, I heard the new teacher will be coming as soon as the harbor opens up and the steamer can come in."

Maggie frowned. "I don't want to even *think* about school," she said. "After all, summer holidays have only just started." But summer wouldn't be the same with Vera sick.

Heavenly Father, Maggie begged silently outside Vera's door. Please show me how I can help Vera. Please use me as you did the little slave girl in the Scriptures—the one who sent Naaman to your prophet so he was cured of leprosy. Show me how to help Vera, please. In our Savior's name. Amen.

Maggie approached Vera's bed. Her cousin lay flushed against the white sheets, and some of her pretty blond hair had fallen out with the fever. Maggie fingered the brush on the bedside table that was filled with clumps of Vera's hair. "Vera," she whispered. "It's me, Maggie. Can you hear me?" She touched Vera's crimson cheek. "You're so hot. Why do they put this blanket over you when you're burning up?" With a swift yank, Maggie pulled the heavy quilt away from Vera. Then, wringing out a cloth from a pan of water next to the bed, she stroked it across her cousin's forehead and down her neck and shoulders. "That's better," she crooned. "You'll feel better when you're cool."

Vera's eyes fluttered. Her parched lips mouthed a word.

"What is it, Vera?" Maggie sat on the bed, straining to hear.

"Ice."

"You want ice?" Maggie asked.

"So hot."

At that moment, Aunt Selina entered the room.

Maggie jumped up. "She spoke to me! She said, 'Ice.'"

"Ice," Vera muttered again. "Hot." Her eyes rolled up, and her body began to shake.

"Grace!" Selina screamed. "Come quickly. Vera's having a fit! Oh, God!"

Maggie's mother raced into the room. "I'll hold her down while you put a towel in her mouth. She'll bite her tongue."

Maggie watched helplessly as Vera's body stiffened, her back arched, and her arms and legs trembled violently.

"She's too hot," Maggie stammered. "Make her cool. She wants to be cool."

"Leave us be, Maggie!" Ma ordered. "She's having a convulsion."

Maggie backed away, suddenly sick to her stomach. "She begged me to give her ice." Tears filled her eyes.

Ma and Selina encircled Vera's twitching body with the quilt, trying to calm her down. Soon the awful jerking stopped, and Vera fell limp, unconscious again.

Ma looked over at Maggie. "Don't cry, Maggie," she said gently. "Please go home. We don't want you to see Vera like this."

Maggie went downstairs and out the door. Back on her porch, Sirius was sleeping in a patch of sun, one big paw clamped over his bone.

Maggie sat on the steps. I asked God how to help Vera, and when she opened her eyes she asked me for ice. But where could Maggie find ice? Once winter was over, there was no way to keep food or water cold. Meat and fish were preserved by sprinkling them with salt and drying them in the sun.

Maybe freshly drawn well water would be cool enough for Vera. That was the coldest water they had . . . except for the sea. Maggie took the water pail from behind the door and trudged down the hill to the well.

Bonnie Bay lay before her, glittering in the late morning sun. Out by Killock Rock Island, where the rocky cliffs enclosed the harbor like outstretched arms, the great iceberg shimmered, like an uncut blue jewel.

Ice, thought Maggie. Cold, clean, freshwater ice.

DANGER AT THE ICEBERG

MAGGIE RAN DOWN THE DIRT ROAD TO THE DOCK where Pa tied up their red dory. She tossed the pail into the flat-bottomed boat and climbed in. The small boat tipped with her weight, and she was suddenly aware of the swells and whitecaps in the harbor. She looked out at the iceberg. Vera wanted ice, and Maggie was going to get it for her.

The boat teetered as Maggie scrambled to the stern. A box containing some of her father's fishing tackle and knives was tucked under the seat. Among the tools Maggie found a small chisel. Good! She would use that to chip the ice from the iceberg.

She untied the ropes that secured the dory to the wharf and settled into the center seat. Maggie took hold of the long, wooden oars and began rowing out into the harbor. I'll have to row gently so I won't disturb the berg, Maggie thought. Sometimes icebergs would turn in the water, or large chunks of ice, called *growlers*, might break off from the mother berg. If either of these things happened, huge waves could swamp boats much larger than her little dory. Maggie shuddered as she thought about what it must have been like for the *Titanic* to have collided with that iceberg.

The harbor waters were like a giant sea monster, whose deep breaths raised and lowered the boat. The waves were heading toward shore, against Maggie, slowing her progress away from the wharves. Gradually, though, the shoreline receded. The sounds of church bells drifted on and off the breeze, and Maggie could make out the distant spire and the figures of the parishioners, some walking, others riding in carriages, as they left Sunday worship.

The waters around her had lost their aqua blue color and were now almost black. Threatening clouds were beginning to darken the sun. Maggie turned to see how far away the iceberg was, and gasped. There it was, looming just ahead, like a giant phantom. If the *Titanic*, as big and powerful as she was, could be destroyed by an iceberg, what chance could her little red dory stand against this massive, monstrous berg? I can't go any farther, Maggie thought with sudden desperation. I shouldn't have come.

But the ice. She had promised Vera she would get ice.

What was that eerie sound? Almost afraid to look, she scanned the choppy water. It was a growler, about the size of a barrel. The smaller iceberg made deep grumbling noises as it bobbed in the waves to the port side of the boat. I'll chip off ice from that, Maggie decided. It's closer and safer! She pulled hard on her right oar, turning the boat to port, then began rowing with all her strength. Waves were hitting the dinghy broadside, and the gunwales dipped into the frothing surf.

I'll be swamped, Maggie thought. But then the growler was alongside, and Maggie managed to pull in the oars and grab the chisel, and she leaned over to the floating mound of ice.

The small iceberg bobbed away each time

Maggie stabbed at it. Then, finally, as the dory turned slightly in the mounting surf, the ice stayed close enough for Maggie to proceed.

She chiseled at the ice, grabbing the loose pieces and tossing them into the pail. For one terrifying moment, Maggie almost toppled overboard as the dory rose and dropped in the swells. She shifted her weight to the center of the boat to stabilize it, but it made it harder to chip the precious ice floating alongside. All the while, Maggie tried to ignore the wind that whistled around her and the sound of breaking waves.

Maggie knew she should head back. When her pail was almost full, she set it carefully under the seat and rowed hard on one oar, pointing the bow toward the safe shore of Bonnie Bay.

Maggie had thought that rowing back would be easier since the wind was in her favor. But she had not counted on the turning tide. The harbor waters had become a swift current that tugged against her. Arching her body, she pulled the long oars with all her strength. Slowly, slowly, she moved closer to the village. Her arms felt as if they would break.

I won't look, she thought. I'll just keep rowing until I'm back. One, two, three . . . Maggie counted. When she reached twenty-two, she looked around. To her dismay, she had drifted away from the village and was heading toward the huge rocks that jutted out from the cliffs. Bearing on her right arm, she headed the bow toward the village wharves. She could see several people gesturing to her from the docks.

She could make out Otto and Cliff and a third dark form. Good! They'll help me. Without thinking, she let go of the oars, stood up, and waved desperately at them. Then, suddenly, a huge swell lifted the boat, knocking Maggie into the bottom of the dory. The pail of ice tipped, and Maggie grabbed it, setting it upright again. Nothing could happen to that ice. She had promised Vera. . . .

Maggie reached for the oars. They were gone! She searched the pounding waves and saw them drifting away.

Now what would she do? How stupid! she thought helplessly. Again, she stood up in the boat and screamed, "Help me!" The boat tipped, and she sank down onto the seat again.

Otto and Cliff were climbing into a dory that was even smaller than Maggie's. Could they make it in time to help her? The wind gusted wildly, and clouds gathered and boiled in the sky. Maggie's boat drifted closer to the rocks.

Then Maggie saw the third dark form on the docks leap into the water, making a faint splash.

It was Sirius. He was coming to help her.

"Go back, Sirius," she called. "Go back!"

But the huge dog had disappeared into the tossing waves. Surely he would drown in the wild surf. Ocean spray and salty tears drenched Maggie's face. In her eagerness to help Vera she had risked her own life, and now her dog's and her friends' lives, as well.

She scanned the black water. She could see Sirius's huge head as he rose with the swells. Maybe he *could* help her.

"Come on, Sirius!" she cried.

The dog was approaching the boat, his shoulders heaving as his great paws reached out through the water.

Scrambling to the front of the boat, she gathered the bowline into her arms. "Here, boy," she called. "Take the line and pull me in." Treading water at the side of the boat, Sirius grabbed the length of rope in his mouth and headed toward the shore.

Maggie could feel the boat turn and tug. It had been almost impossible for *her* to row against the strong tide. Could Sirius do it?

Maggie spotted Otto and Cliff's dory bobbing in the waves. She sank to her knees on the floor of the boat and watched as the dog struggled with his heavy load. "Please, God, save us," she whispered, "and save my dog."

Sirius had pulled the boat away from the rocks, and now they were headed in the direction of the wharves.

Finally Otto pulled up to her and grabbed the line from the dog. "Go back," he ordered the panting Sirius, who treaded water, his eyes never leaving Maggie.

"Go!" Maggie yelled. "Good dog!" Sirius turned obediently and swam ahead. Maggie whispered, "Thank you, Lord."

In the stern of Otto's skiff, Cliff took hold of Maggie's bowline while Otto rowed to shore with long, sure strokes.

As they pulled up to the docks, Cliff climbed out and tied the red dory to the wharf while Otto hitched up his own boat. Sirius staggered onto the shore and shook himself, sending off a spray of seawater.

"Come on, Maggie," Cliff said, holding out his hand. "You nearly did yourself in on that trick."

"Don't be tongue-banging her," said Otto, giving Cliff a stern look. "She's feeling bad enough."

"I'm sorry. I'm *so* sorry," Maggie said as she climbed out of the boat. "Wait!" She turned back to retrieve the pail from under the seat.

Vera would have her precious ice after all.

NIGHTMARE

"OH, MAID," OTTO SAID, SHAKING HIS HEAD. "YOU gave us a fright. Why did you go out to the iceberg by yourself? Certain, now, you knew the danger." Cliff stood silently by, stroking Sirius.

"I wanted to get ice for Vera. She begged for ice, Otto."

Otto put his arm around Maggie's shoulder. "I know how much you love your cousin. We all do. But we wouldn't want to lose you, either, Maggie."

Maggie avoided his eyes. "I'm sorry. I truly am. I'm sure I'll be in for it when I get home." Sirius lapped her hand, and she dropped to her knees. "You tried to save me," she said, burrowing her face into his wet fur. Sirius licked her face and whined. "You're my bright star dog, and I'm so glad you're all right." Sirius wiggled excitedly.

"We'll walk home with you," Otto said. "Maybe it will be easier to face your ma with us there." He took the pail from Maggie. "Come on, now." He and Cliff started up the road..

Maggie followed them. "My mother's at Vera's, I'm sure," she said. "I've got to go there first, anyway, before the ice melts."

"We wouldn't want that to happen, would we?" Cliff said with a half smile. "Not after all the trouble you went to."

Sirius lumbered along, stopping now and then to shake himself, sending a spray of salt water over everyone.

"He's drying himself off right well," Cliff said with a laugh, "but you're getting even wetter!"

Maggie tried to smooth the wrinkles in her damp dress. Then she spotted the carriage and the horse. Pa was back with the doctor. Maybe Vera would be all right now. She saw Ma in the doorway. Had she already heard about Maggie's expedition to the iceberg?

Otto spoke up first. "We're back safe and sound, with some freshwater ice for Vera." He handed Ma the pail. "How's the maid?"

"Better," Ma answered, looking into the bucket. "Where did you get this ice?"

Maggie cringed. Ma *didn't* know what she had done, but Otto answered quickly. "Maggie had the notion that Vera could use some ice, and . . ." He paused.

Ma's face paled. "The only ice is out in the harbor. The iceberg . . ."

"Oh, there are some growlers from the big berg not too far out," Otto interrupted. "Maggie got hold of one and chipped off a bit."

"We helped her bring it in," said Cliff.

What they said *is* the truth, Maggie thought with relief.

"Anyway, take the ice to Vera before it melts," Otto directed. "No sense wasting it."

Ma nodded. "Come in," she said, standing aside. Her gaze fell to Maggie's wet clothes. "Then you'd better get home and change, Maggie."

Maggie sat on a chair to take off her shoes. Uncle Norm and Pa were drinking tea at the table. Dr. Auld came down the stairs and joined them in the kitchen. "Maggie, Vera's been asking for you," he said.

"She's better, then? I brought her ice."

"You'll be a nurse someday," Dr. Auld said, patting her shoulder. "Your mother said you had tried to cool her down, and you were right, you know. She's come around since we cooled her off and bathed her. Now that we've got healing herbs into her, I think she'll be as right as rain."

Maggie started to fill a tin cup with water from a pitcher.

"No, no, Maggie," warned Dr. Auld.

"We mustn't drink water from the well anymore," said Pa.

"Use the boiled water from the kettle," Uncle Norm told her.

Maggie was puzzled, but did as she was told and added chunks of ice from the pail. "I promised we would bring her ice," she said with a grateful smile at Otto. "And we did."

Vera was propped up against the pillows, her face pale since the fever had broken. Her eyes were closed, and her lashes were dark against her white skin. Her hair was all patches from the fever.

Aunt Selina stood at the window that looked out at the harbor. The iceberg was visible from this spot, as were the reef and the stages. Selina's eyes locked with Maggie's, and then she looked away.

She knows, Maggie thought.

Maggie sat on the edge of the bed. "I have a surprise for you, Vera," she whispered.

The ice tinkled in the tin cup, and Vera tried to sit up. "Where did you get ice?" she asked in a weak voice. Her lips were parched and peeling.

"Out in the harbor. A growler from the big berg. Here," she said gently. "I'll help you." Maggie held the cup to her cousin's lips. Vera drank eagerly.

Ma came to the doorway. "Dr. Auld says that the well water is what made Vera sick. So now we must boil everything to kill the germs. We'll need to find another well."

"Fortunately, most of us only drink hot tea or water from the kettle. That's why the rest of us are all right," Aunt Selina said. "But we're *all* in danger."

"Where can we find another well?" Maggie asked. "There's nothing but rock everywhere around here. We can't dig for water."

"Wish we could attach a pipe to that iceberg," said Aunt Selina. "That's the best water there is."

Her eyes caught Maggie's again. But Maggie was sure now Selina wouldn't tell. Another secret, she thought. Eleven ravens.

"Cool and fresh and right delicious," Vera whispered as she eased her head back against the pillows. Vera's eyes closed, and Aunt Selina motioned for everyone to leave the room. But before Maggie left, Selina caught her hand.

"Maggie, Sirius is a marvelous dog, you know. The two of you did a wonderful deed. Dangerous, but wonderful. No matter what the Rands try to do, we won't let anything happen to that dog." She squeezed Maggie's hand.

"Thank you, Aunt Selina," Maggie whispered.

Back downstairs the men were discussing where they might dig for another well.

"Old man Rand has a well big enough to serve everyone. It's fed by a spring that's on his side of the mountain," said Uncle Norm thoughtfully.

"He doesn't own the mountain or the water," Pa said. "I don't see why we couldn't tap into it somewhere. Rand has enough water for all of Bonnie Bay, but he'd never share it with any of us."

"Particularly *you*." Otto sent a knowing look at Pa.

The words and the look were not lost on Maggie. There's something going on between Pa and the Rands, she thought as she stepped out the back door. Sirius looked up and wagged his tail with loud *thumps* on the porch floor.

Maggie sat on the steps and patted his shiny head. "Why do the Rands hate us so much? There must be a reason, Sirius," Maggie decided, "but no one talks about it."

Maggie thought about those eleven ravens up at the *quidnunc. A secret that will never be told.*

That night, Maggie's dreams were as wild as a stormy sea.

Maggie was in the dory all by herself. There were no oars. Mountainous waves tossed the small boat toward the towering iceberg, which loomed like a ghost.

In the water, her dog held fast to the bowline and struggled to bring her back to shore. Maggie watched in horror as the dog's slick black head finally slipped under the surf and disappeared.

Sirius! Maggie tried to call, but the word was garbled.

Then out of the sea rose a figure dressed in flowing black. Maggie saw the waves ripple and foam and become a rustling petticoat. Above the tumultuous sea, rolling clouds gathered into straggly hair, and two stars in the sky melded and glistened into eyes.

It was Tamar, and she was laughing.

THE LOST TREASURE

Maggie awoke with a start. Her forehead was sweaty, and her heart was beating fast. The old hag who brings nightmares had visited her, and Maggie was certain something awful was about to happen. She struck a match and lit the lantern by her bed. What was wrong? Vera was going to be all right. Sirius was asleep down in the kitchen. Everyone was safe.

I'll wager that Tamar is the old nightmare hag herself—trying to haunt me even in my dreams.

Maggie sank back into the pillows. Today is Monday, and the Rands will go to the constable, Maggie thought. Would they convince him that Sirius is dangerous to sheep? We would never own a dog that would harm sheep. Why, my great-grandfather in Scotland kept sheep. Our people are sheepherders from way back.

Maggie pictured her great-grandfather and his herds of woolly sheep dotting the hills of Scotland. Suddenly, she remembered something. The family brooch! Where was it?

She leaped out of bed, almost knocking over the lantern. Where was her blue dress?

She had taken it off last night and dropped it on the chair. There. Maggie grabbed it and searched for the silver pin. Gone!

Maggie groped under the chair with both hands. The brooch wasn't there. Nor was it on the top of her dresser with her hairbrush and ribbons. Frantically she pulled out each drawer, shaking the contents onto her bed. She rummaged through the clothing, but the brooch was not there.

Had she taken it off and put it back in the velvet box down in the parlor? Maggie took the lantern and tiptoed down the stairs, her bare feet cold on the wooden floor.

The light from the lantern made strange shadows on the walls and ceilings. As she passed the kitchen she heard Sirius snoring loudly.

Maggie found the velvet box and opened it. It was empty. Maggie sat on the floor. The Celtic brooch was the most precious thing her family possessed—a reminder of their heritage and past generations—and now she had lost it.

Sirius yawned in the parlor doorway.

"Come here, boy," Maggie whispered. The dog lumbered toward her, his tail swishing back and forth happily. "Oh, what have I done?" She put her arms around him, burrowing her face into his white star. She cried softly. Sirius licked her hair and nudged her head with his nose.

Maggie wiped her eyes. She must retrace every step she had taken yesterday. Church. Vera's house. The well. The road to the harbor. The pin could have fallen off anywhere.

Sirius reached out with his forepaw and patted her leg. "I can't go looking for it now. It's still too dark," she said. "Oh, where could the brooch be?"

Sirius stood up and cocked his head at Maggie. He wagged his tail slowly.

"Maybe . . ." Maggie got up and held out the velvet box to Sirius. "Yesterday you smelled this, Sirius. Do you remember the pin?" The dog sniffed the container.

Maggie led Sirius into the kitchen, continuing

to hold the box out to him. "Go get it, Sirius," Maggie commanded, and opened the kitchen door. Sirius wagged his tail but looked puzzled. Again, Maggie held the box to the dog's nose. "Here," she directed. "Go to the dory. The boat! Go get the pin. *Go get it.*"

Sirius started through the door, then paused.

"Good boy. Go get it. Boat," Maggie ordered in a stern voice, pointing out the door. Finally Sirius trotted onto the porch, down the steps, and disappeared into the early morning shadows. The wind was southerly, and the salty smell of the ocean drifted across the porch. A light shone in a window at Vera's house, and Maggie wondered if the brooch could be there somewhere. If it was, Aunt Selina would bring it straight over. But what if it had fallen into the sea? Then it would be gone forever.

Maggie sat down at the kitchen table and laid her head in her arms. Surely Sirius didn't understand. How could she send off her loving and gentle dog with such harsh words? After all, it was her own fault that the brooch was missing. Why had she worn it in the first place? For some stupid sentimental reason she felt that the brooch might bring some kindness or good fortune—for Vera. What did Pa say about superstition? "Foolishness. We are the masters of our own lives and fortune."

Maggie decided that as soon as it was light she would search the church and the well.

She got up and put the teapot on the stove and opened the damper. A hot cup of tea would make her feel better. The day was brightening, and she looked out the door to see if Sirius was back yet.

Noises came from upstairs. Ma was getting up. How could Maggie face her mother and father and tell them she had lost their most prized family possession? She tucked the velvet box in the pocket of her nightgown.

"You're up early, Maggie," said Ma. She glanced at the stove. "What a good child. You've lit the fire and have tea brewing." She viewed the glass barometer on the wall. "Good weather today." She stood back to look at her daughter. "Is something wrong?"

"No." Maggie hated to lie. But she might find the brooch once it was light enough outside, so

Ma didn't need to know about it. Not yet.

"Don't worry about Vera. She's going to be all right." Ma smiled at her gently. "See? The Lord heard your prayers, my dear."

Maggie nodded and turned away quickly.

"Let's have some biscuits and bake apple jam. Just you and me."

Bake apple. Maggie's favorite, and used only for special occasions. Ordinarily, it would have been a sweet moment to be having tea with Ma, but Maggie was so worried about the brooch, it was hard to pretend everything was fine.

Ma studied her daughter's face. "What's wrong, my child? Can't you tell me?"

Maggie turned to the window again. "It's . . . Sirius. I don't want to lose him." The morning sun, in a haze of sea fog, now cast a golden glow over the harbor. Poor dog. How could he have any idea of what Maggie had sent him to do?

"Here, maid," Ma said comfortingly. "Here's the tea. You get the biscuits, and we'll plan some way to fight for Sirius. We'll do everything we can to keep him here with us. But if not, we can send him to my sister in Corner Brook. He'll be safe there."

"No. I'll never see him again if he's sent away,"

Maggie said vehemently. She already had a plan if the worst were to happen. "I'll find a way to keep Sirius."

Maggie brought a tin of biscuits out of the cupboard and set them on the table. She turned back to the window. Sirius was already at the gate and heading back to the house. Maggie hurried to let him in.

"Speak of the Devil," said Ma, "and he appears."

"Come in, boy," said Maggie, holding the door open. Sirius had done his best. She must not expect a dog—even a dog as smart as Sirius—to understand and solve her problem.

"Everyone in the family takes off their shoes when they come into my kitchen," Ma said with a laugh, "except for that animal." She pretended to frown. "Off with your boots, you old thing," she commanded. Sirius wagged his tail.

"Come here, boy," Maggie said gently, tapping her thigh. Sirius went over to Maggie and stretched out his great head over Maggie's open hand. He dropped a wet and slimy object into her palm.

Sirius had found the silver brooch.

SECRET AT THE *QUIDNUNC*

M AGGIE KNELT AND HUGGED SIRIUS. "MY SWEET Sirius," she whispered. "You found it!"

Sirius whined softly and lapped Maggie's face.

"You slobbery, wonderful dog," she laughed. "Thank you, thank you."

"What did Sirius bring you?" Ma asked. She turned Maggie's hand in hers. "The brooch?"

"Oh, Ma, it must have fallen off my dress yesterday," Maggie explained, standing up. "This morning when I realized it was gone, I sent Sirius to find it—and look. He did." Tears trickled down her cheeks. "That's why I was so sad. I thought it was gone forever."

Ma looked in wonderment at the silvery pin, then to Maggie's tearstained face. "It's all right, my dear," she said, gathering her daughter into her arms. "It would have been a tragedy for sure, had it been lost. But it's all right. We have the brooch, and you don't need to feel bad anymore." Ma examined the pin. "The clasp is bent, so it doesn't hold the pin tightly. Pa can fix it."

"I'm sorry, Ma. I thought it had fallen into the sea when I went out . . ."

Ma wiped her daughter's face with a handkerchief. "It's all right, Maggie." She motioned Maggie to the table. "Now, you eat and don't worry so much."

Sirius put his paw on Maggie's knee. Maggie gave him a biscuit. "Here, my clever star boy," she said. "You are such a good dog." Sirius took the biscuit and ate it loudly under the table.

Maggie spooned some rich cream from the tin her mother opened and stirred it into her tea. The tea did taste good and soothing. Then, remembering the velvet box, she pulled it out from her pocket. "I was going to tell you, Ma," she said, placing it on the table. "But I wanted to look for it first."

"I understand, Maggie."

Maggie could tell from her mother's voice that the issue was closed.

"Now, if we can only find a way to get some water into our house. We can't be going out to that iceberg again. So we have to boil this water for now—for a long time—before we drink it. I'm tired of pumping out of that well and carting water back here every day, anyway," Ma said, spreading bake apple preserves onto a biscuit.

"It would be right nice to have water piped directly to our kitchen sink," Maggie agreed. "Real modern—like the Rands."

"Well, the Rands *do* seem to have a lot. But much of their wealth is ill-gotten," said Ma with a nod. "He's charged off too many expenses to the fishermen here, and things are about to change."

"How, Ma? What do you mean?"

"Pa and I think you are old enough to know. You're almost thirteen, and you're a responsible girl. But, you mustn't tell anyone."

Was she about to hear the secret that caused those knowing looks between Pa and Otto? Maggie leaned forward eagerly.

"You know how Pa went to St. John's last month to visit his brother? Well, Uncle Bert has a boat for sale. Five of the families here in Bonnie

Bay are going to buy it. We've worked, hoarded, and saved, and now we're about ready to make our dream come true. Pa will be the skipper. Everyone else will have an equal share in the profits. We won't have to work for old Rand anymore." Ma put her fingers to her lips and stifled a laugh.

Maggie was astonished. "Do the Rands know about this?"

"Oh, goodness, no. Not yet," said Ma, chuckling. "It's going to be a big surprise!"

"But I heard Otto say that Howard Rand is angry at Pa. I'm sure he's heard something about it. That's why he's acting so mean about the sheep."

Ma nodded. "Could be, Maggie. He's been more than his usual nasty self lately." She played with a crumb on the starched white tablecloth, then looked up. "It is hard to keep a secret like this—especially in Bonnie Bay."

Pa came into the kitchen, his dark hair tousled from sleep. His hair was the exact shade of brown as Maggie's—with hints of gold in the sunlight. People said Maggie resembled her father—except she had inherited the same unusual amber eyes of her mother. Pa was already dressed in wide, dark jeans held up with embroidered suspenders. Like all the fishermen in Bonnie Bay, he wore a long-sleeved *gansey*, a sweater from the Isles of Guernsey. Even when the days were warm onshore, it was cold on the Atlantic.

"So now you know, Maggie girl. How about it? Won't you be happy to have your pa a proper ship's captain?"

"Yes, Pa, but what about the Rands?"

"There's not a thing they can do about it. Just a few more weeks and a new boat will be down in the harbor. I'm naming it *The Grace*, for your ma." He put his hand on Ma's shoulder and kissed her cheek.

"Is it brand-new?" Maggie asked.

"Well, it looks like new," Pa answered. "And the engine purrs like a contented cat and leaves hardly a wake. It's a nice-lookin' boat and will serve all of us well." Pa poured some tea and sat at the table. "But, remember, we don't talk about it yet."

"I won't tell," Maggie promised. "But I think old Rand already knows."

"That would explain why he's concentrating on Sirius. He doesn't really believe that our dog would hurt anything. But he's out to make life miserable for us," Pa agreed. "He's not about to let anyone steal his lines."

Hearing his name, Sirius crawled out from under the table and sat at Maggie's feet. His tail thumped the floor rhythmically.

"Now we've got to figure out what to do about our boy here, should the constable show up." Pa scratched Sirius's head.

"Oh, Pa, the Rands have probably talked to the constable already. They won't try to shoot Sirius, will they?" She saw a quick look pass between her father and mother. "They can't." Her voice rose. "You can't let them hurt my dog!"

"There, now, Maggie. I'm sure it won't come to that," said Pa, reaching for her hand.

She pulled away from him. "No, it *won't* come to that." Maggie jumped up, squeaking the chair. Sirius yelped and bounded out of her way.

Maggie raced up the stairs and put on some old clothes—a flowered calico dress that she had almost outgrown. It came down only to her boot-tops and would make it easier to climb among the rocks. Hastily, she tied a ribbon around her curly, unkempt hair. No time to wash up, she thought. I've got to hide Sirius.

She bolted down the steep stairs and almost fell over Sirius, who was waiting at the bottom. "Rope. I need a long length of rope, Pa." She stuffed her bare feet into her old boots.

"What are you up to, Maggie?" Ma chided. "Calm down."

"No. I won't. I'm taking Sirius away myself—where no one will find him!"

"All right, my child," Pa agreed. "I have rope out under the porch."

Maggie, her father, and Sirius went out into the cool air. Maggie couldn't see over the hillside, where the road wound up to her house. Howard Rand might be on his way with the constable right now. "Please hurry!"

Her father retrieved a coil of rope from beneath the steps and handed it to her. "What are you planning to do, Maggie?"

"I'm going to hide Sirius. Come on, boy," she said, tying the rope to the dog's collar.

"Maggie, wait." Ma came out to the porch, holding a plate full of meat. "Let him eat this first."

The dog's tail swished wildly, but he waited for the command. "*Eat!*" Ma said, and Sirius lunged for the food. "He'll need water, too." Ma went back inside and returned with a bowl of cool, boiled water. "Do you want me to come with you?"

Maggie shook her head. "No one must know where Sirius is." No, she wouldn't tell *anyone*. After all, even the big secret about the new boat wasn't really a secret anymore.

Sirius had gobbled up the meat and was lapping the water. "Come on, Sirius," she urged.

The dog looked up, water streaming off his jowls, and she tugged on the rope. She would come back for more food and water later, but now she just had to get Sirius away from there.

"Hiding Sirius is like concealing a whale in a puddle," Ma called out. "Are you going to Beachy Cove?"

"I'm not telling you. That way you won't have to lie if someone asks," Maggie said over her shoulder as she and Sirius headed behind the house and into the thicket. To anyone watching, it would look as if she were heading through the woods to Beachy Cove, a deserted harbor, several miles away.

Actually, Maggie had considered hiding Sirius there. Few people ever went there. It was a long, arduous walk through heavy spruce thickets. However, it was easily reached by boat, and people might expect that's where he'd be. Besides, how could she feed him and watch over him if he were so far off? No, Maggie had another plan. A better plan.

Out of sight of the houses, Maggie turned and led Sirius up the overgrown back pathway to the *quidnunc*. Sirius jogged along happily, not at all annoyed by the rope leash. It was getting hot, and mosquitoes buzzed around them, but Maggie didn't pause until they had reached the first outcropping of rocks. "Sit!" she commanded Sirius, tying the rope loosely to a scrub tree. Sirius sat. Maggie crawled out onto the cliff and looked over the rocks. Below, the colorful houses of Bonnie Bay, with their crisscrossed stick fences, looked unreal, like a small child's drawing. She gasped when she saw three people heading up the path to her own house. One of them was short, and she recognized Tamar. "It's Howard Rand and Tamar," she said out loud. "And the constable must be with them." Squinting, she could just make out that both Howard Rand and the other large figure were carrying rifles.

Maggie shuddered and scrambled back to her dog. "We got you out just in time," she whispered. "They came with guns! How could they do this?" She untied Sirius from the tree, and they continued up the overgrown narrow path to the *quidnunc*. Then she sat down on the rocks and pushed on Sirius's rump until he sat down, too. "Now, I know this will be hard for you," she said gently, "but, trust me, Sirius, and you'll be safe down there." She pointed to the mossy ledge below. Maggie slid her way downward over the smooth boulders. "Come on."

Sirius held back, but as Maggie slipped farther down the rocks, the rope tugged at his collar. He felt his way with his paws, taking unsteady steps toward Maggie.

"There. Good boy." Once she and Sirius were safely below in the crag, Maggie surveyed the secluded mossy ledge. No one would see Sirius with the thicket surrounding him. The sun beat down on the balsam and spruce needles, making a sweet scent around them. "There's a nice place here for you to lie and warm yourself, Sirius. Now, come here, boy." She tugged at the rope, and Sirius followed her to the small hidden cave. "See? If it rains, you'll keep dry here." She laid the old blanket from her copy house on the floor of the cave. Sirius sniffed at it, then lowered himself onto the blanket and watched her. Maggie untied the rope from his collar. "I don't want to tie you up," she said sadly. "But you mustn't follow me. You must *stay*."

Maggie crawled out from the cave. Sirius rose.

"No, Sirius!" she said sternly. "*Stay!*" She leaned into the cave and put her arms around him. "You've got to *stay*. I'll be back."

Maggie coiled the rope and tucked it into the cave. She made her way up the ledge and, halfway up, she looked back. Sirius had emerged from the cave and was watching her, his tail wagging slowly. Then he sprang to the rocks to follow her.

"No!" Maggie repeated. Sirius backed down to the ledge. "Oh, Sirius, how can I make you understand? You've got to *stay*. I don't want to have to tie you up in this lonely place."

Once more, Sirius lunged for the cliff.

"*No! Bad dog,*" she shouted. "*Stay, you bad dog.*"

Sirius paused and looked hopefully up at Maggie as she scrambled to the top of the *quidnunc*.

"*Stay!*" Maggie waited, praying she would not need to tie him up.

Sirius clambered down to the mossy ledge. He watched Maggie with sad eyes, his tail motionless as he obediently stood by the cave.

SIRIUS IS MISSING

Maggie waited at the top of the *QUIDNUNC* for a short while, unsure if she should leave Sirius untied. Sirius was an obedient and trusting dog, Maggie told herself, but to leave him here alone made her uneasy. And she felt bad about shouting such hard commands. She peeked out over the rocks. Sirius lay at the opening of the cave, his head on his paws.

Sirius had always obeyed in the past—faithfully—even when the choice was difficult for him. Pa had been the one who had taught him obedience. When Sirius was a puppy, Pa once placed a ham shank in front of him and sternly commanded the dog not to touch it. Sirius eagerly jumped for the tempting bone. "No, bad dog," Pa scolded, swatting him on the rump. Maggie had run to her room and shut the door. "It's for the best," Ma had said. "You'll see. The dog needs to be trained."

Sirius learned quickly. Even now he would wait for the command to eat before lurching into his food.

And what a hardworking dog he turned out to be. Last winter after a sleet storm, the horses were not surefooted on the slippery ice, so Pa hitched Sirius to a sled and set off across the frozen harbor to get some firewood that he had cut during the previous summer. Sirius had pulled one heavy load of wood across the bay, then slumped in the snow, exhausted.

Maggie objected strongly. "Sirius will break his back with all that wood."

Pa fashioned a makeshift sail on the sled to lighten the load. On the next trip the sail filled with a steady breeze, and Sirius trotted across the ice ahead of the sled, seeming to enjoy the adventure. Maggie smiled as she remembered her black dog on the white surface of the harbor and the packed sled in full sail. What a good dog Sirius was.

Now Maggie felt sad as she peered down at

her dog. But it's for his own good, she thought. What else could she do? The constable and Howard Rand were probably still at her house with their rifles.

Maggie leaned against a rock and gazed up at the fleecy clouds overhead. "Dear Father in Heaven," she whispered, "I thank you that Vera is better and that you heard my prayers. Now I'm praying for my dog. I'm sure he was a gift from your loving hands. He's been unjustly accused, and they're waiting down there with guns. You know he never hurt Tamar's sheep. Sirius is a good dog. Please save him from being killed. Perhaps you have some plan—some test for me." The Bible said God never gives people more than they can bear. "I can't bear to lose Sirius. Please, spare him, Lord," she finished.

The sun was almost directly overhead in the china-blue sky, and a jay was chattering in a tree. The scent of balsam and spruce soothed Maggie. If only she could stay right here forever and leave all her troubles down in the village. But it was time to go back.

She peeked down the ledge once more. Sirius

was sprawled on his side, sleeping, his tongue hanging out from the side of his mouth.

"Good dog," Maggie whispered. "I'll be back later."

When she reached the bottom of the hill, she turned into the thicket and made her way out onto a rocky path. A half mile farther and she reached the fork where the main roads converged.

She headed up the slope toward her house.

Ma opened the door before Maggie reached the gate. "They were here," she said. "Howard Rand, Tamar, and Joey Harper, the constable."

"Did they have guns?"

"Yes, my child, they did. But Pa told them that Sirius was gone and they should leave us alone."

"Did they ask where he was?"

"Pa said he was gone and that was that. But they warned us that if Sirius should come back to Bonnie Bay, they would have to shoot him."

Maggie started. Maybe she should have tied Sirius up after all. What if he came home? What if someone found him?

"Don't worry right now," Ma said. "We'll find a way. Joey Harper didn't sound happy about all this, and he was trying to make some sort of peace here. He knows Sirius. He knows how good he is and how he helps us. And he knows that dog would *never* harm a sheep. Pa may go talk to Joey with Uncle Norman and Aunt Selina. They've promised to stand up for Sirius. So have Uncle Jabe and Aunt Gertrude. Maybe the constable will listen if the Rands aren't there."

"Tamar will be watching to see where I go—where I've hidden Sirius."

"Well, you just keep on the watch for *her*," warned Ma.

It would be hard to keep this secret. Maggie was sure of that.

For the next couple of days Maggie kept on the lookout for the Rands. Tamar, who usually stayed on her side of the village, was now playing every day with Annie Kelly. The Kellys lived only two houses away from Maggie—and closer to the hidden path to the *quidnunc*. Annie had always been Maggie's friend and classmate, but now Annie and Tamar had become "thick as thieves," as Ma had put it. Being a friend of the rich Rands was something to be desired, especially by Annie, who admired Tamar Rand's clothes and large, modern home. "Some friend she turned out to be," Maggie sputtered to her mother.

Unlike most of the trim houses and neat gardens in Bonnie Bay, the Kellys' place was always "in a clobber"—shabby and untidy. The walks around the small green house were overgrown with grass and weeds.

Maggie would have to be cautious about passing the Kellys' on her trips to feed Sirius, especially now that Tamar was spending so much time there. The back way to the *quidnunc* was rocky and tight with overgrown spruce and bushes, and carrying heavy parcels of food up there was difficult. Sirius had faithfully stayed at the cave and wasn't straying from where she had left him. Maggie tried to see her dog early every morning, then again later in the day. Each time Maggie arrived at the top of the *quidnunc* and looked down, she could see him waiting, his eyes glued to the spot where he knew she would appear. Then Sirius wiggled in excitement, his tail wagging madly, like a sail in a gale. When Maggie finally descended to the ledge with her parcel of food, the dog greeted her with sloppy kisses, soft barks, and whines.

One morning, less than a week after she had hidden Sirius, Maggie concealed a satchel of food and a leather flask of water in a large carpetbag. She headed up the road and was passing the Kellys' house, when she heard a familiar voice.

"Where are you going?" It was Tamar. She must have spent the night with Annie.

"For a walk," Maggie answered.

"With that big bag?" Tamar said. "Isn't that too heavy to take on a walk?"

Maggie flicked her head toward the Kellys' ramshackle house. "Do you live here now?"

"No," Tamar answered icily. "Annie and I are planning a party." Annie appeared on the porch and sauntered to Tamar's side.

"Why are you having a party?" Maggie was unable to control her curiosity.

"My sister, Marie, is coming home in two weeks with her baby," Tamar bragged.

"His name is Benjamin, and that makes Tamar an aunt," Annie piped up.

"We're having the christening party at the church." Tamar smiled. "But *you* and your family are *not* invited."

"I wouldn't go if I were," Maggie shot back. Hoisting the carpetbag over her shoulder, she continued on her way. This time she walked farther along the narrow, winding path to Beachy Cove. Were the girls whispering about her, or was that the southerly wind rustling through the needles of the spruce trees? No doubt they were spying to see if she was going to Sirius.

Maggie lunged into the tuckamore, a low clump of trees. Then she crept through the bushes toward the old trail up to the *quidnunc*, dragging the carpetbag behind her. Halfway there, she peeked over the cliff and could see Tamar and Annie sitting on the porch steps.

Humph! she thought. Tamar wouldn't have a thing to do with Annie Kelly until Sirius disappeared. She wants to be close to my house so she can watch me—and taunt me. Well, I couldn't care less about her and her silly old party.

At the top of the cliff she started her slide down the smooth, rounded boulders to the cave.

The ledge where Sirius usually waited was empty. "Sirius," she called as she slid herself down to the outcropping. "Sirius!"

There was no welcoming bark. Only silence.

THE HIDDEN SPRING

MAGGIE DROPPED THE BAG OF FOOD ON THE GROUND and frantically searched the cave and the surrounding scrubby trees. There was no sign of Sirius.

His food bowl was empty. His water bowl was tipped over. How long had he been without water? That was it. The poor dog was thirsty and had gone looking for water.

Maggie searched for tracks or signs that Sirius might be close by. Had he gone home? Most likely he would have taken the trail she had used to bring him up, and yet there were no clues to where he might have gone.

"Sirius!" she called—then louder, "SIRIUS!"

A faint rustle in the distant bushes caught Maggie's attention. Running toward the sound, she could make out a black form through the

trees. It was Sirius. He barked when he saw her
and whacked the bushes with his tail. Then he
bounded out of the brush and trotted toward
Maggie's outstretched arms.

"Where have you been, you silly boy? You're
all wet," Maggie exclaimed, feeling the fur on the
dog's neck and chest.

Sirius pawed her leg and then headed into the
brush again, turning back to see if she would follow.

Maggie trailed Sirius through the under-
growth to the base of another hill that stretched
up on the north side of the *quidnunc*. "Where are
you taking me?" she asked.

The dog sprang ahead of her, stopping
momentarily to give her time to catch up, then
climbed up more rocks, through some woods
where Maggie had never been before. In places,
the thicket was so dense, she could hardly make
her way through, but suddenly they came to a
small clearing, and Maggie stopped. What was
that sound?

Maggie followed Sirius behind several boulders, and the noise got louder—a gurgling, gush-

ing sound. There, through a gap in the mountain rocks, a sparkling brook bubbled its way over the stones and tumbled in little waterfalls to a cave farther down the hill, where it vanished from sight.

"Water!" Maggie cried. "You've found water! The brook must come from a spring way up on the mountain." Maggie did a little jig. "Wait until Pa hears about this. He can come up here and pipe this water down to our houses." She could hardly wait to tell her folks. She crouched by a prancing Sirius. "I know you were thirsty, poor thing," she murmured as she snuggled her face in the damp star on his chest. "You knew you mustn't come home, so you went looking for yourself. And see what you found. You're my good dog," said Maggie, hugging him again. "My clever star dog."

Maggie led Sirius back to his hiding place and filled his bowls with food and fresh water. Eager to get home, she grabbed the empty carpetbag and climbed to the top of the *quidnunc*. Marcus Kelly, Annie's father, was standing on top of the cliff.

Maggie gasped.

"So here's where your dog is hidden," Marcus said. "Thought no one would find him, eh?" He reached down to help Maggie up the rocks, but she didn't take his hand.

"He's not bothering anyone," she muttered, brushing herself off.

Marcus spit on the ground. "Sirius is not *bothering* me, but I'm sure Howard Rand will be *bothered* when he knows that dog is still around." Marcus smiled his toothless grin.

Maggie tried to stay calm. Now that Marcus knew where Sirius was, he might blabber it to everyone—especially if he had drunk a little too much. Even worse, he'd probably try to win over Howard Rand by telling him where she had hidden her dog.

She decided to keep Marcus on her side. "Rand won't be bothered if you don't tell him," Maggie said sweetly. "And you wouldn't do that, would you?"

"No, maid, I wouldn't tell that binicky old fool," he said. He reached out and patted Maggie's shoulder. "Don't fear, child. I can keep a secret, you know."

Maggie smiled and said, "Thanks, Marcus. My pa will be owing you for that." Perhaps if Marcus thinks he'll get something for his silence, he might keep his mouth shut. And maybe Pa *could* make a deal with him, she thought. "I'm going down to tell him right now how helpful you've been."

"Ah, good, Maggie. And ask him to mix up some calabogus. I'll be over later." Marcus sat down against a tree.

"I'll be sure to tell him. Good-bye, Marcus." Maggie waved.

Maggie pushed through the tight saplings. Pa will find a way to keep Marcus quiet, she thought. If Marcus says one word about Sirius to Annie, she's certain to tell Tamar.

She stepped out into the road and walked casually past the Kellys' house.

She entered her kitchen, slamming the door behind her. Ma and Pa looked up from the kitchen table in alarm.

"Pa!" she shrieked. "Marcus Kelly saw Sirius up on the *quidnunc*."

"So *that's* where you've been keeping Sirius," said Ma.

"He'll tell Rand, I know he will," Maggie raced on.

"Calm down, Maggie," Pa said calmly. "Tell us what happened."

Maggie related her encounter with Marcus. "I think he might have been drinking."

Ma shook her head. "Poor Lucy."

"If he tells Annie, she'll tell Tamar and—"

Pa interrupted. "Maybe we should move Sirius out to Beachy Cove after all."

Maggie nodded. "I'll do it early tomorrow. Before the sun is up."

Ma got up from the table. "Don't worry, Maggie. Things will work out." She poured water from the kettle into a teapot. "Oh, we're out of water again. All I seem to be doing these days is carrying water up from town, or boiling it." She sighed. "Can you get some water for me, Maggie?"

"Water!" Maggie cried. "I was so busy worrying about Marcus, I forgot to tell you that I found water way up on the *quidnunc*."

"You *what?*" her mother and father exclaimed together.

"Well, Sirius really found it. His water was

gone, and he went into the woods. He showed me the way. It's beautiful water, bubbling and gurgling through the rocks. And there's lots of it!"

"Maggie, that's wonderful news," said Pa, jumping up. "We can get Norm and the others up there and pipe that water right down the hill behind our house. There might be enough pressure to pipe it straight *into* the house." He pulled on his boots. "Let's go up now and you can show me."

"But, Pa, what about Marcus?"

Her father frowned. "Hmm, well, I have an idea that might work. Marcus isn't a bad person except when he drinks too much. There may be a way we can get him on our side—a way to keep him sober and give him something to look forward to at the same time."

"Oh, balderdash," Ma groaned. "Reuben, you know you can't tell what's going on in the mind of a squid. And Marcus is a squid. You never know if he's moving backward or forward."

"Now don't *you* get into a hobble, too," Pa replied. "I'll take care of Marcus."

"When I left him on the *quidnunc*, I told him he could come over here for some calabogus later," Maggie said hopefully.

Pa burst out laughing. "You know the way to that man's heart," he said. "For now, Grace, you get busy making some calabogus—that's the one sure way to lure him here." He laughed all the way out the door. "We're having Marcus Kelly for tea," he called.

Ma chuckled and shook her head. "Marcus for tea—that *is* a laugh." She opened the kitchen dresser. "There's rum and molasses here. I'll borrow some spruce beer from Aunt Gertrude. The calabogus will be ready when you come down." She waved to Maggie and Pa. "This should be *some* tea party!"

"Come on, Maggie," said her father. "Take me up to that wonderful spring. Then I'll have a long talk with Marcus Kelly."

SIX RAVENS

Marcus was still asleep under the tree where Maggie had left him.

Maggie pointed down to Sirius sleeping by his water bowl.

"Shh," Pa said, "we don't want to wake either of them. First, show me the spring."

Maggie led the way through the tight wall of spruce limbs, up the back cliff of the mountain.

"Oh, Maggie. You're takin' me as far as ever a puffin flew," Pa said, pushing his way through the mass of trees. "How did you find your way up here? No wonder the spring has never been discovered." After climbing around several boulders, Pa stood by the gurgling brook. It seemed even more brim-full and sparkling now as it wound noisily through the rocks.

"Beautiful," Pa murmured. He bent down and scooped up the cold water in his cupped hand. He sampled the water and smacked his lips for any doubtful taste. His face broke into a radiant smile. "Perfect water, Maggie. It's running so fast through these rocks, I'm sure it's as pure as the driven snow. There's nothing around here to contaminate this supply." He hugged his daughter. "To find this hidden place and this spring—you've done well, Maggie."

"Sirius found the water," Maggie reminded him.

Her father nodded. "We'll start piping this down to our houses right away. There's enough pure water here for all of us."

Maggie and her father headed back to the *quidnunc*.

"Come on, Marcus." Pa shook the sleeping man. "Time to come for tea. We've got some planning to do, you and I."

Marcus mumbled, and his eyes fluttered open.

"Get up, Marcus," Pa insisted. "We have some calabogus waiting for you at our house. But first I've got an offer for you."

Marcus blinked his eyes. "All right," he said. "Let's go down for tea."

"Come on, now." Pa pulled Marcus to his feet.

Marcus looked around. "Now how the dickens did I get up here?" He saw Maggie. "Ah, now I remember. You and that dog."

Maggie looked anxiously at her father.

"It will be all right, Maggie," Pa said gently. "Marcus and I have some business to talk about. Don't you worry." He put an arm around Marcus, and the men walked unsteadily through the tuckamore and down to the road.

Maggie looked down at Sirius. He was washing his paws with his tongue. I won't let him know I'm here, she decided, slipping away from the edge. Shadows fluttered overhead. Six black birds soared above her. Ravens? Crows? Whatever they're called, it's still *six for crying*, Maggie thought.

Back at the house, Pa and Marcus disappeared into the parlor and closed the door. The kitchen smelled sweet, like molasses. Ma was mixing the calabogus mixture with a mundle—a large wooden spoon with which she usually stirred soup.

Maggie wrinkled her nose. "Ugh! How can anyone drink that? It makes me want to yuck."

"Well, molasses is good for you," Ma acknowledged, "but I don't think it's a great idea to give any more liquor to that man in there. Why, he's as thin as an eggshell, and just as fragile." Ma set the mundle on the sink.

"And as dirty as duck's puddle." Maggie held her nose. "I don't suppose he's changed his clothes in months." She wondered what kind of plan Pa could possibly have for Marcus.

Her thoughts were interrupted by a thunderous sound that echoed off the mountains and rattled the windows. "What was *that?*" She ran out onto the porch. The sky was clear and blue. Maggie looked toward the harbor. "The iceberg is breaking apart," she called. People gathered down on the wharves to watch as the great mound of blue ice shattered and collapsed.

"The harbor looks like it's full of sailboats," said Ma.

"I'm going to tell Vera."

Vera was set up in the front room on a cot by the window. She wore a lace bonnet to cover her thin hair. "I heard the iceberg," she exclaimed. "When it's all gone, the harbor will be open. And I'll be better soon, Maggie. We can play together and gather berries, and—"

"And Pa will get the new boat . . ." Whoops! Did Vera know about the boat? Maggie had said she wouldn't tell, and now she'd gone and broken her promise.

"New boat?" Vera's eyes widened.

Maggie tried to undo her mistake. "You know how Pa always wanted a new boat. Maybe dreams will come true this summer. Maybe."

She sat on the cot next to Vera. "I dreamed about Tamar," said Maggie. "She rose out of the sea like a monster."

Vera laughed. "When I was sick, I dreamed I was flying. I was high above the ground and I could look down on Bonnie Bay."

"Pa says someday everyone will fly in those new aeroplanes. Can you imagine?"

"I'd fly to Toronto," Vera stated. "That's where I'd go."

"I'd fly to the States," Maggie said. "To Boston— to a big hospital, where I'd become a nurse."

"Wherever we go, we should go together," Vera said, taking her hand. "Let's always be together."

"Yes," Maggie agreed. "Always."

Maggie had lunch with Vera: Aunt Selina's ham and pea soup—so thick, a spoon could stand straight up in it—and freshly made Methodist bread, full of plump raisins. Maggie whispered with Vera about the new water source that Sirius found and made her promise not to tell.

When Maggie got home, Pa and Marcus were still in the parlor, and the calabogus sat untouched in the kitchen. Ma was in the old rocking chair by the stove, knitting on a crazy quilt afghan she had started last fall. It was a conglomerate of leftover yarns and colors, giving it a patchwork appearance—not unlike the plots of land and multicolored houses of Bonnie Bay. If Maggie could fly over Bonnie Bay, she was sure the ground below would look like Ma's afghan.

Maggie put her ear up to the closed parlor door but could only hear the low murmur of voices. They'd been in there for over an hour. What could they be talking about for so long?

Maggie sat down at the table. "Ma, have you

heard about the big christening party for the Rands' grandchild?"

"Yes, I have. Their daughter Marie is coming by steamer and bringing little Benjamin the Saturday after next. With the iceberg gone, they should be able to get right into the harbor. It's too bad her husband can't come, but I hear he had to go up to the Labrador."

"Tamar said *we* aren't invited to the christening party."

"Reverend Dobbs asked me to help with refreshments," Ma said.

"Are you going to make refreshments when you're not even invited to the party?"

"Well, it's the Christian thing to do." Ma's fingers danced with her yarn and needles. "Maybe it will help make some peace here."

How could Ma be so mild about this? The Rands had threatened to kill Sirius, and now Ma was making refreshments for them? It didn't make any sense.

Just then the parlor door opened. Pa came into the kitchen with Marcus behind him. Pa gestured for Marcus to sit down. "Grace, would you pour us some tea, my dear?"

Ma put down her knitting. "Tea?" she asked.

"Yes, Grace. Just tea, please," Marcus replied.

Maggie looked over at Marcus. His thin, unshaven face was swollen, and his eyes were red. She couldn't believe it. Marcus Kelly had been crying!

THE GALE

Maggie never did find out just what Pa had said to Marcus that day in the parlor, but from that day on, Marcus showed up at the Wellses' door first thing every morning. Pa and Marcus worked together fishing, mending nets, and patching up the wharf for the new boat.

It was busy on the stages now that the iceberg no longer blocked the harbor. Some of Rand's crew had already begun heading out to sea. Soon *The Grace* would be docked in Bonnie Bay. Uncle Norm and Otto were investing in the new boat and looking forward to being on their own at last.

On Monday, before heading to the *quidnunc* to tend Sirius, Maggie went to Art's store for Ma. Cliff was there with Otto.

"How are you, Maggie?" Cliff asked. He was

dressed in the coveralls and boots of a fisherman. "We're going out jigging this morning. Want to come?"

"No, thanks," she said. She had no time to sit around in a boat while Otto and Cliff jigged for codfish all morning.

"It's nice out there today," said Otto. "Not a flobber. Not a wag of sea."

"But I hear on the wireless there's a big nor'easter heading up the coast," said Art. "It's battering Nova Scotia and should get *here* by week's end."

"Maggie, did you hear that the law against dogs has been passed?" Otto asked. Maggie shook her head. "Yep, it's official. Only sheepherding dogs are allowed in these parts anymore."

How could this happen? Now Sirius was in more danger than ever.

Cliff sensed her dismay. "Come with us, Maggie," he coaxed.

"I'm helping Ma," Maggie answered abruptly, and handed Art the list of groceries.

"Bones?" Art asked, looking at the list. "Your mother wants bones? What for? I thought your dog was gone."

"He *is* gone," Maggie replied hastily. "Ma's making soup."

Art nodded and gathered the groceries.

"Well, Maggie," said Otto, "I hear there will be a new teacher in the fall. She's due to arrive on the steamer."

"For a while it looked like there would be no one to teach next year," Art said. "Wouldn't *that* be just too bad?"

Maggie nodded. "I wonder if she knows she'll be teaching kids from first grade to eleventh grade all in the same classroom." She grinned. "No wonder teachers leave all the time."

"Well, they're not trained teachers," Otto replied. "They're just young ones from other parts of Newfoundland who've finished their grades and have no jobs yet."

"From what I've heard, Cliff here should be teaching school himself," said Art as he wrapped some bones in brown paper. "You're a bright lad, my boy."

Cliff blushed and looked down at the floor. "Aw, I'm just a blear—an ignorant coot from Labrador," he muttered. "I don't have *real* schooling."

"You can read better than anyone I know. Once the new teacher gives you some tests, we'll have a better idea where you stand academically." Otto nodded at Art. "Care to take any bets on the grades this boy will make on his exams?"

"He'll do right well," Art said. "Maybe you'll go to McGill and become a doctor, Cliff."

"Or Harvard," Otto added.

"Someday I'm going to Boston," Maggie interjected.

Art plunked a can of cream on the counter and began adding up the prices to put on the Wellses' bill. "You're just a girl, Maggie. You'll stay here and marry a fisherman, and that'll be your life."

"I will go to the States and become a nurse!" Maggie countered. "Dr. Auld said I'd be a nurse someday. Those were his very words." Yes, that's exactly what she would do. Maggie grabbed the parcel from the counter and headed out the door.

Maggie heard footsteps behind her. "I'll walk with you, Maggie." It was Cliff.

She paused and waited for him to catch up. "I thought you were going jigging."

Cliff laughed. "Once Otto gets talking, who

knows when we'll get out there. Here, let me carry your parcel." Maggie handed it to him gratefully. "I miss seeing your dog," he said, stuffing the package under his arm.

"I miss him, too." She wondered if he would ask where she was keeping Sirius. Then what would she say?

"You know, if you could prove he's a sheepherding dog, no one could harm him," Cliff said. "The new law exempts sheepdogs."

"But he's not a sheepdog. He's never been trained to herd sheep. Besides, the Rands are the only people with sheep here. I can just imagine the Rands letting my dog work their sheep," Maggie snorted.

"Just a thought," Cliff said with a shrug. "He's such a clever dog, Maggie."

As much as she liked Cliff, Maggie couldn't tell him where Sirius was hidden. For a while the only sound was the trudging of their footsteps along the dusty road. From the corner of her eye, Maggie looked at Cliff. He had an angular jaw and high cheekbones. His blond hair had a way of slipping over his forehead when he moved. This was a right nice-looking boy, Maggie decided.

"Maggie, wait!" Otto ran up behind them. "Your pa got a wireless message from St. John's," he said. "Art just wrote it up. Here." He handed an envelope to Maggie. "It has to do with the new boat."

Maggie nodded. "Pa's at home," she said, "waiting on Marcus."

Otto smiled. "Those two are as thick as tar lately. And Marcus has never looked so well. What did your pa do to him?"

"I don't know," Maggie said. "I'll bring this straight home. Pa will be eager to see if the boat is ready." No secrets from Otto. He was already part of the crew. And surely Otto had told Cliff, since he seemed to know what they were talking about. But how she longed to see Howard Rand's face when *The Grace* pulled into Bonnie Bay.

As if reading her thoughts, Cliff said, "Mr. Rand will be more than huffed when the rumor about the new boat becomes a reality. He's already worried about losing his crew."

"He knows it's not just a rumor. That's why

he's throwing such a big party after the christening." Otto laughed. "He's not one to fling money around without a reason." As he started back to the wharves, Otto winked at Cliff. "We'll go fishing when you get through with Maggie."

Maggie flushed and looked down at her dusty boots. "You don't need to walk with me," she said softly.

"I want to," Cliff answered. "I've been thinking about you and Sirius. You must feel awful about losing him."

"I do," she said. "Pa said he'd talk to Joey Harper—that's the constable—but he's been too busy. Now he'll go off to get the new boat and he won't be here to help me hide—" She stopped. She had almost given away her secret. "I mean . . . I'll still have to wait for him to speak to Joey Harper."

They reached Maggie's house. Pa and Marcus were sitting on the porch. She thrust the message at her father. "It's for you."

Pa ripped open the envelope and read the note. "It's ready!" His words rang out like a trumpet. "We're off to St. John's today. If we can get to

Whale's Gulch, we can take the steamer." He turned to Cliff. "Please, my boy, go back to Art's store and ask him to send a wireless ahead for me. We've got to get ready right quick if we're going to make that ship."

Cliff nodded, waved to Maggie, and ran down the road. "I'll help Otto get the wagon ready," he called over his shoulder.

Marcus leaped from the chair. "I'm going with you."

"Of course you are. You're one of the crew now, Marcus. Go pack your duds. We'll be gone a few days."

So, he's one of the crew, thought Maggie as she watched Marcus trot up the road to his green house. That must have been part of Pa's plan for Marcus all along.

For the next hour the Wells family hustled to help Pa get ready for the trip. Maggie wrapped up some bannock bread, bake apple jam, and a bottle of switchel. Ma gathered warm, clean clothing and packed it into a canvas bag.

Otto and Cliff arrived with the horse and wagon. "Cliff said you'd probably need a ride down to the steamer," said Otto. "You'll be coming *back* on that new boat!"

"Watch for her comin' around the neck," Pa said, giving his wife a quick hug and kiss. "We'll be back by week's end. Maggie, watch over your ma. Help her out, maid."

Maggie put her arms around her father and tried to hold back her tears. "Oh, Pa. I hope nothing happens to Sirius while you're gone."

"Everything will be all right, my child," he whispered.

"Pa, I saw six ravens—six of them, for crying."

Pa took his daughter's hand. "Maggie, the ravens—crows—they don't foretell your future, my child. I've told you before, we make our own futures. The Bible says there's a time for everything under the sun. A time to laugh and a time to cry; a time to mourn and a time to skip about and dance. That little verse about the ravens—or crows—is just a reminder, that's all."

"Will we ever feel safe and laugh again?" she asked.

"You'll laugh again, my Maggie. I promise you." He turned to Otto. "While I'm gone, maybe you can start digging the trench for the spring."

"Aye." Otto nodded. "We'll have that water piped to the houses before autumn comes."

Pa turned to Cliff. "And you, Cliff, keep an eye on Maggie for me."

Marcus loped down the road, his arms loaded with a seabag. "I'm comin'. Wait up for me." Lucy and Annie followed him partway, then stood at the bend in the road, waving. Marcus climbed on board the wagon, and Otto clicked the reins. The wagon started slowly toward the village.

"Good-bye, Pa," Maggie called.

Overhead, a flock of gulls soared high, calling loudly to each other, and Maggie whispered the old proverb: "'When gulls fly high, a gale is nigh.'"

Then she recalled Art's words: "There's a big nor'easter heading up the coast. . . . Should get *here* by week's end."

SHIPWRECK!

Grace is ready to go. She's a beauty.
Leaving Thursday. Will be home before storm.
Don't worry.
Reuben.

MA CLAPPED HER HANDS. "PA IS ON HIS WAY HOME," she said. "He left yesterday. This is so exciting, Maggie. All our dreams are coming true. Pa is master of his own vessel."

Didn't Art say the gale battering Nova Scotia was a threat to Newfoundland? "Would Pa dare start out with the threat of a storm?" Maggie asked anxiously.

"He's so eager to get back, he just might take that chance," Ma said. "But he knows these waters like the back of his hand. He'll pull into port if it gets rough. He'll be just fine."

Just then Lucy Kelly knocked on the door. Annie stood behind her. "When will my Marcus be back?" Lucy called out. "There's a storm brewing."

"They headed back yesterday." Ma showed Lucy the telegram, then invited them inside. "Look at the weatherglass," she said, pointing to the glass teapot-shaped object on the wall. "There's no sign of a storm yet." The blue-colored water was low in the spout, indicating high pressure and fair weather.

Somewhat relieved, Lucy slumped into a chair and looked around. "I don't know how you keep everything so tidy, Grace," she said enviously. "I can never get things right at our house."

"I'm sure you've been busy helping the Rands out with the christening party," said Ma, setting the kettle onto the stove.

"Yes. The Rands did hire me to help. They are so excited about the baby. First grandson, you know. So Howard Rand has invited everyone in town, let me tell."

"Well, not everyone," said Annie as she settled herself into the rocker.

Ma just laughed. "No, we haven't had the honor. But I'm making some cookies for the affair."

"Really?" said Lucy and Annie together. Lucy spotted Grace's afghan on the back of the rocker and reached out to touch it. "Real nice and soft," she said, "like a baby blanket."

"The colors *are* pretty," Ma agreed. "I want to finish it up in time for the christening."

Maggie forced herself to stay quiet. How could Ma give the Rands a present after all the trouble they'd caused!

Lucy seemed surprised herself. "That's right kind of you, Grace," she said. "And I don't know what Reuben has done with my Marcus, but he's a different man lately." She looked briefly at Annie and then went on. "He hasn't touched a drink since their talk."

Ma took the whistling kettle to the sink and filled the teapot. "I'm glad to hear that, Lucy. Marcus is a good-hearted man. He just has a problem with Newfoundland rum."

"And beer, and calabogus, and anything else

available," Lucy muttered. "Well, whatever Reuben said, it seems to be working. I've never seen Marcus get up so early as he has been lately. He washes up, gathers brishney from the yard for the morning fire . . ."

"And lately he's been polishing his boots with tallow and oil," Annie added. "I always had to do that for him."

"Miracles, that's what it is," said Lucy.

"Reuben *does* have a way with words." Ma poured the tea. "Here, Annie, sit with us. Maggie, bring out some bake apple tarts and cream. We'll have a nice visit while our men are gone."

Maggie did as her mother asked, but she couldn't help being upset with Annie. Hadn't she clearly taken sides with Tamar against her? Was Ma really making the blanket for the Rands' grandchild? She plunked the food on the table and sat down.

Lucy looked out the window. "I can see the smoke from your chimney falling down. And the clouds are moving fast from the east."

"'When the wind is in the east, 'tis neither good for man nor beast,'" quoted Annie.

Ma changed the subject. "Lucy, would you drop by tomorrow and pick up the food for the party? Hopefully the afghan will be finished in time."

"I'll be here," Lucy said, nodding. "Do you think Reuben and Marcus will be back by then?"

"Yes, I think so," Ma answered. "The storm's not due to hit until later in the weekend. The steamer is coming in tomorrow morning. It should get here before the storm."

"The cats were very playful today," Lucy mused.

"That's right," Annie said. "It never fails that we have a bad storm when they act that way."

Maggie dropped her teacup with a clatter into the saucer. "Please stop it!" She knew well the old saying that when cats are playful, they are said to "gale up the weather." "That's all foolish superstition. *Pishogue!*" She glanced over at the weatherglass. Had the water in the spout risen in the last minute?

Lucy followed her glance. "I knew it," she exclaimed. "The storm is closer than we thought. Marcus and Reuben will head straight into it. And so will the steamer that's bringing the Rands' new grandchild. There's trouble ahead, I just feel it in my bones."

"Nonsense," said Ma, sipping her tea calmly. "Reuben knows enough to get to port in a storm, Lucy. Now calm down and drink your tea and enjoy the afternoon."

Lucy drank the rest of her tea, but her eyes kept wandering to the window. Finally she stood up and thanked Grace. She and Annie took their leave.

Once they had left and were out of sight, Maggie took her daily hike up the *quidnunc* to feed Sirius.

At supper time, Otto and Cliff appeared at the door. They had been digging the trench for the pipe from the mountain spring, and Ma had promised them a boiled dinner of salt beef, cooked in a huge pot with cabbage, turnip, carrots, and potatoes. Ma had also filled a muslin bag with yellow split peas and hung it inside the pot to cook with the other ingredients. Peas porridge was one of Maggie's favorite dishes.

"Smells good in here," Cliff said as he removed his boots. "Boy, the wind sure is picking up out there."

"Yep, there's white horses on the bay," Otto added, referring to the whitecapped waves.

"Take a look at the weatherglass," said Maggie.

The spout was now half full. "I hope Pa gets to port before the storm hits."

"Don't worry, maid. The storm's comin' on us as fast as you'd say 'trapsticks,' but Reuben's been a seagoing man all his life. He'll be all right."

As night set in, the four of them sat at the table with bowed heads. By the light of the kerosene lamp, Otto asked the blessing and ended with the plea, "Heavenly Father, watch over our friends and loved ones on the sea this night."

"And please watch over Sirius, too," whispered Maggie. "Amen."

The storm raged that night. The rain lashed at the windows, and branches snapped off of the crab apple tree. Maggie woke up in the middle of the night to the sound of gale winds that carried the roar of the sea. She prayed for Pa and Marcus and wondered about Sirius all alone up on the *quidnunc*. She buried her head into her pillow, so her mother wouldn't hear her crying.

A little while later, Maggie went downstairs. Ma sat at the kitchen table, a lantern and open

Bible in front of her. She pointed to the weather-glass. The blue liquid had overflowed the spout and spilled into the metal tray that hung below.

"Oh, Ma," Maggie said. "It's such a bad storm."

"And it came on us so quick." Ma got up and put more wood into the stove. "It's a fast-moving gale. The worst will be over by daylight," she said. "We've weathered bad storms before."

"But we've always been together," Maggie said. "Do you think Pa found a safe harbor?"

"Of course he did," Ma said, drawing her daughter into her lap. "Try not to worry too much. You need to show your faith, Maggie. God hears prayers, you know."

Amid the thrashing of the wind and rain, Maggie heard a faint scratching sound. "What's that?" Maggie ran to the door. The wind took her breath away as she peered out into the darkness.

"Sirius!" she cried.

Soaking wet and shivering, Sirius crept into the kitchen.

"Poor old beast," Ma exclaimed. "Bring him close to the fire, maid." She pulled a woolen blanket out of the closet. "Rub him dry, Maggie, while

I get him some food." She shook her head. "Oh, poor dog."

Maggie realized at that moment how much her mother loved Sirius. The blanket was a good one, freshly washed in precious water and dried on the clothesline. But it didn't matter to Ma. Maggie draped the blanket around the dog, rubbed him briskly, and crooned to him.

"My sweet Sirius, my bright star dog. I shouldn't have left you up there in the storm. I'm sorry. I'm so sorry." The dog whined softly and slapped his wet tail against the floor.

Ma placed some leftover boiled beef in front of him. "Eat," she said gently. Sirius lapped at the food, looking now and then at Maggie, who continued to alternately rub him and hug him. After eating, the dog curled up on the blanket by the fire and fell asleep, snoring softly.

"We'll keep Sirius here until we're sure he's well. After all, he's been out in the gale all night," said Ma. "But we'll have to be right careful who comes into the house."

"I hope he didn't catch cold." Maggie said, petting Sirius's damp head.

Ma tucked the blanket up around Sirius. "He'll be all right, Maggie. He's used to snowy weather, and it's not really cold out. Just windy and wet."

Maggie and Ma stayed in the kitchen all night. Sirius slept soundly by the stove. The rain began to let up, but the gale winds continued to howl around the house and whistle through the chimney. When Maggie opened the front door for a moment, gusts of deafening wind assaulted her. With force, she pushed the door shut and bolted it.

Maggie thought about Pa—hopefully in a harbor, and not somewhere out there on the wild sea.

Ma stood at the kitchen window. She voiced Maggie's very thoughts. "I'm sure he's put into a safe port by now."

In midmorning, Uncle Norm banged at the door. He was covered from head to foot in a southwester raincoat; wisps of hair were plastered to his face, and his eyes were shadowed by dark circles. He must have been up all night, too, Maggie thought.

"What's wrong?" Ma asked.

Maggie held her breath, her eyes fixed on Norm's anguished face.

"Is it Reuben?" Ma's voice trembled.

"No," he answered quickly. "But there's bad news. The steamer is sinking off Killock Rock with almost a hundred passengers on board!"

A STAR IN THE STORM

Maggie grabbed her slicker from a peg by the door and followed Ma and her uncle down to the village, onto the harbor neck. Most of the townsfolk had already gathered there.

Through the mist and fog Maggie could see the ghostly form of the steamer as it listed on the rocks offshore.

"She had turned to head into the harbor, but lost her engine," Uncle Norm hollered over the sounds of the crashing surf. "The breakers carried her into the rocks."

A bright signal light blinked from the ship. "They're taking on water!" yelled a familiar voice. "Get a boat out there!" Howard Rand was running around, gesturing madly at the crowd.

Four men in a large rowboat were already

heading for the ship. Maggie watched as a huge wave lifted the bow, turned the boat right over, and scattered the rescuers in the black, churning waters.

Farther back in the harbor, more boats were being launched—this time to save the rescuers.

"My daughter is out there—and her baby," yelled Howard Rand.

The foundering ship continued to send flashing signals—bright lights that penetrated and hung in the thick fog. The steamer bounced in the water, lopsided, tilting into the rocks. Maggie saw Constance Rand and Tamar clinging to each other, unmindful of the wind raging around them, their total attention on the tottering ship. Maggie took hold of Ma's hand.

Uncle Norm joined the fishermen on the rocky beach.

"What will they do?" Maggie asked her mother. "There must be a way. The ship is so close. If the tide went out, maybe . . ."

"No, maid," said Ma, gripping her daughter's hand. "The tides are higher than usual because of the storm and the new moon. This is very bad.

But there must be *some* way to help those passengers and crew."

Maggie thought of Ma's old proverb, "'The old moon in the arms of the new; bodes no good for me nor you.'"

"A breeches buoy!" Uncle Jabe yelled over the wind. "They're signaling for us to help set up a breeches buoy."

"What's a breeches buoy?" Maggie asked.

Otto stood nearby. "It's a lifesaving device. Maggie," he explained. "A rope line is set up—a pulley—between the shore and the sinking ship. The breeches are usually a pair of canvas britches attached to a circular lifesaver, you see. Each passenger gets into the britches and is hoisted to land over the water." Otto pointed out to the ship. "But how to get a line out there, and bring one back, is the question that would stump the Devil himself." He shook his head. "There's no way in these waves."

The fog was lifting and the sky was brighter, but the clearing westerly wind strengthened, creating mountainous breakers.

Lucy and Annie had arrived and were huddling

together against the wind. Their faces were strained as they looked out at the steamer.

Uncle Norm and Cliff climbed to a high rock overlooking the water and set up a huge wooden foghorn. Cliff pumped a set of bellows, and Norm forced the handle down. The loud horn bellowed, echoing across the water.

"I hope they can hear our signals," Otto said to Ma. "Norm is telling them that we're still trying to send boats out there. See? Cliff is pumping the bellows, and Norm is blowing the horn with the handle. It's the only way we can communicate with the ship right now."

"They're setting up the breeches buoy on their end," Howard Rand yelled. He was reading the flashing signals from the ship. "We've got to bring back their line."

"Aye," someone shouted. "But *how?*"

"Small boats can't make it in these waves." It was Uncle Jabe's voice.

The deep horn sent this message to the foundering ship.

Otto moved close to Maggie and spoke with his cupped hand to her ear. "We both know how to get a line out there and back, don't we, Maggie?

We both know a way to save all those people."

Sirius.

Sirius could swim to and from the boat—that's what Otto was trying to tell her.

"No!" Maggie screamed, clapping her hands to her ears and shaking her head.

"What's wrong, Maggie?" Ma asked.

"No," she repeated. "Not Sirius! He'd drown in those waves."

Otto nodded. "Yes, he might, Maggie."

"Oh, my child," said Ma. "I forgot about Sirius. He may be the only one who can help."

This is all a dream, Maggie told herself. I'll wake up and see Sirius asleep in the kitchen, and Pa having tea at the table, and no storm. Everyone is safe. This is just a dream.

But it was no dream.

"Maggie, you've got to make the right decision. You know what to do, my child," he said.

"Even if Sirius could do it and didn't drown, it wouldn't change anything," Maggie cried. "Howard Rand would still have him shot tomorrow. I know he would."

"Everyone will speak on Sirius's behalf, Maggie."

"But the law . . ."

Another boat had been launched. Maggie prayed the boat would make it to the steamer. But it rose too high on the great waves, and the men headed back to safety.

"Marie! Marie!" Constance Rand screamed as the steamer shifted farther against the rocks. "Someone help them!"

Maggie looked over at Tamar, who clung to her mother, crying.

"Where are you going, Maggie?" called Ma as Maggie headed away from the beach.

"I'll be back soon," Maggie yelled. She raced along the rocky shore. Her throat ached, and tears blinded her as she flew up the hillside to her house.

"Come, Sirius," she said, bursting into the kitchen

Sirius sat up and yawned. Maggie knelt down to hug him.

"You've got to help the passengers," she whispered in his ear. "This is something you have to do, Sirius." She sat back on her knees and stroked his smooth head. "It will be hard, but God will guide you, my sweet dog."

Maggie got up and opened the door. "Come on, boy," she said, pointing outside.

Maggie brought Sirius down to the shoreline, where Howard Rand was standing with Otto, Uncle Jabe, and the others.

"Good girl, Maggie," said Otto. "That was no easy decision, let me tell."

Ma put her arms around her daughter. "Oh, Maggie," she said. "My brave girl."

Someone cheered. *"The dog can bring the ropes!"* Somebody else yelled, *"That dog can swim better than a fish!"*

Maggie looked up at Howard Rand. "My dog will swim out to the steamer," she said. "He'll bring the ropes for the breeches buoy."

After a moment, Howard Rand turned to the men on the shore. "Don't just stand there!" he hollered. "Get our end of the buoy set up while this dog takes the line out there."

Cliff pumped the bellows while Norm signaled the ship that the dog was coming.

Back on the beach, Sirius barked and pranced, his fur ruffling in the wind.

Rand read the return signals from the steamer.

"They know he's coming," he said. "Send him off, Maggie." He handed her the end of a coil of heavy rope that had been knotted into a loop.

Maggie led Sirius to the edge of the water. She put the rope to his mouth. "Go to the boat, Sirius," she commanded, pointing to the water. "Go bring them the rope." Sirius took the line in his mouth and circled around Maggie. He sat down. "Go!" Maggie pointed again. "Go to the boat!" She pulled on Sirius's collar. Sirius rose and circled Maggie. He stepped into the water, then looked up at her.

"Go to the boat. Bring the rope to the boat. Good dog!"

Sirius plunged into the surf, his legs paddling fiercely, his ears floating around his great head. Maggie held her breath as her dog disappeared into the breakers.

"There he goes!" yelled Howard Rand, raising a telescope to his eye. "I can see him."

Maggie watched the coiled rope unwind. Then she lowered her head and prayed. "Please watch over him," she begged. "Help him save those people—and please bring him back to me." Ma's hand was warm on her shoulder.

Lucy and Annie stood nearby. "Don't worry, Maggie. He'll be all right," Annie said. "He's a brave, amazing dog."

"The coil has stopped," someone yelled. "The dog's gone!" Groans rose from the crowd.

Maggie closed her eyes, trying to shut out the sounds and the shouting and the horn. "Wait! There he is! I can see his black head!" Howard bellowed again, the telescope glued to his eye.

Maggie opened her eyes, relieved to see the cable line unwinding again.

"Is he almost there?" came a shout.

"Can you see him?" Constance Rand tugged at her husband's arm.

"Aye," Howard Rand shouted. "God bless him! He's at the boat!"

The crowd cheered again.

"What's going on now?" Constance pleaded.

"They've taken the rope from him, and they're giving him the other cable," Rand answered. "He's on his way back."

"Come on, Sirius!" Maggie cried. "Good dog. Bring us their line."

The wind howled around the waiting crowd.

"Where is he now?" Ma called.

"He's gone," Lucy moaned.

Howard scanned the surface of the water. "I can't see him. He can't fail now!" He swung around. "Where's Maggie Wells? Get her down here," he ordered. "Call your dog again, Maggie. He knows your voice. He needs to know where you are. Everyone else, not a yap out of you!"

Maggie drew away from Ma and walked to the edge of the water. "Sirius!" she called through her cupped hands. "Come to me, boy. Bring me the rope." Maggie searched for her dog's black form.

"Sirius!" The wind carried her cries out onto the foaming water. "Please come to me, boy," she begged. "Come on, Sirius. Come, boy!"

Suddenly, out of the rising breakers, a form rose and fell with the waves.

Then there was Sirius staggering on the slippery rocks. With the rope clenched tightly in his teeth, he was heading straight for Maggie.

Maggie dashed into the cold surf and grabbed the line. She and Sirius stumbled to shore, where the fishermen took the rope, connected it to the pulleys, and began the rescue.

Cheers echoed over the howling winds and the breaking sea, and resounded against the cliffs. Ma raced to Maggie's side and wrapped her coat over her daughter's wet slicker. The crowd clustered around Maggie and Sirius.

Maggie dropped to her knees. Laughing and crying, she embraced Sirius, who lay exhausted and shivering at her feet.

"Oh, my good, sweet Sirius," she crooned. "My own wonderful star dog."

FIVE BLACK BIRDS

MAGGIE AND SIRIUS SAT CLOSE TOGETHER ON A boulder and watched the rescue begin.

After speaking with Otto and Cliff, Ma, Lucy, and Annie came over to Maggie. "We're going back to the village for warm blankets," Ma told her. "Cliff is bringing back Otto's buggy so we can take passengers back to town."

"They'll be right cold and wet," said Lucy.

"Why don't you come home with us, maid?" Ma asked. "I'll get the fire going, and you can change your clothes."

"No," Maggie answered. "I want to be sure Marie and the baby get back safely."

"All right." Ma tucked her coat around Maggie. "I'll bring you a blanket, too, my child."

Annie waved. "We'll be back a-once," she promised.

Maggie pulled half of Ma's coat over Sirius. "There, boy. I'll keep you warm. You're *such* a good, clever dog." He slapped his wet tail on the rock, then leaned against her, panting.

The sun had finally emerged from behind the clouds, but the howling wind continued to churn up powerful waves. Otto attached the pulley and cable to a stout tree, high up enough on the hillside to keep the rope above the water. Since there were no canvas breeches anywhere, someone brought a sturdy chair from town for Otto to attach to the cables of the rescue buoy.

"It'll be a risky trip across those waves," Maggie heard someone say. "The passengers will need to be strapped in tight."

"Between us and all harm," another voice added.

"Thar she goes," called Uncle Jabe. The pulley moved the chair out over the waves toward the foundering ship.

The chair trembled and shook in the wind. When it arrived at the steamer, someone reached out and drew it onto the deck.

"Women and children first," Howard Rand ordered. Tamar and her mother held hands and waited close by his side.

The chair headed back with its first passenger. "It's a woman," Maggie said to Sirius. "See her skirt flipping in the breeze?" As the chair came closer, Maggie could see a rigid young woman gripping the arms of the chair as it swung over the breakers. "It's not Marie," said Maggie.

When it reached the shore, Uncle Jabe and Art pulled the chair down while Otto unfastened the straps that encircled the woman. As she slipped off the seat, a look of relief swept over her face.

"Where's my daughter and her baby?" Constance Rand cried. "Are they all right?"

"She was terribly frightened," the young woman answered. "She wanted someone else to try the chair first. I'm sorry."

The chair was promptly sent back to the ship to another waiting passenger.

Tamar Rand clutched her father's arm. "Is it Marie this time?"

Howard put the telescope to his eye. "It is! They're strapping the baby to her."

"Oh, please, good God, let them get to shore safely," Constance Rand prayed aloud.

As the chair moved forward, the cable dipped

with the wind and weight, dropping the passengers dangerously close to the waves. Marie screamed as the great waves dashed against her feet. Tamar and her mother echoed her cries with cries of their own.

Maggie jumped up and ran to the water's edge. Sirius followed, barking at the chair as it lurched closer and closer to shore.

When Marie and the baby were finally pulled safely to the ground, another cheer went up from the crowd. The Rands all raced to Marie's side. Otto unbuckled the straps as Howard Rand helped his oldest daughter from the chair. He gathered his daughter and grandson into his arms.

Otto turned the chair back toward the ship where more passengers were waiting impatiently.

"Come on, boy," Maggie whispered to Sirius, heading back to the boulder. "Marie and her baby are safe now."

Ma had returned and was looking for her. "Here you are, Maggie. I've brought you this warm rug, my child."

"Oh, Ma," Maggie protested as her mother wrapped the heavy blanket around her. "This is the quilt from your bed . . . your wedding quilt."

"No matter," Ma answered. "It's all right."

Lucy and Annie walked up with the young woman who came first on the breeches buoy. "This is Nancy O'Brien," Lucy said.

"She'll be our new teacher come fall," Annie added.

"A very *brave* teacher," said Ma.

"I'm glad you're back safe and sound," said Maggie.

"Thanks to you and your dog," Nancy said, patting Sirius, who sniffed at her wet shoes. The girl seemed not much older than Maggie herself.

Howard Rand and his family were climbing into their wagon to head home. But the rescue was far from over.

Someone brought a kettle of thick ham and potato soup to the rescue scene, and Ma filled two tin cups for Maggie and Sirius. Ma set the cup down in front of the dog. "Eat," Ma commanded.

Sirius couldn't fit his nose into the cup. He looked down at the tin bannikin—then tipped it over with his paw, spilling the soup onto the rocks. His tail wagged as he ate the meat and potatoes first, then licked up the liquid.

Maggie ate her own hot soup. She hadn't realized how hungry and cold she was.

The rescue continued throughout the afternoon with the chair traveling back and forth over the water. The boat quivered with the motion of the sea and waves and slipped into deeper water.

"Hurry! Hurry!" was the constant call. "There are still many souls out there."

Everyone, including Ma, was busy with the rescue, bringing blankets and soup, and taking the passengers back to warm houses where they would spend the night.

Maggie curled up inside the quilt, with Sirius across her feet. The rest of the day and evening became a blur in Maggie's mind as the roar of the waves lulled her into a fitful sleep. She heard the cheers, like some distant music, as each passenger reached safety. The rescue team worked tirelessly, finally bringing the crew and captain of the steamer safely to land.

It was dusk when the shouting and cheers finally subsided. Someone carried her to a wagon. She could hear a familiar voice urging the horse forward. But she was too tired to see who it was.

After a bumpy ride, Maggie was helped from the wagon and led into her cozy kitchen. Ma helped Maggie put on a nightgown that she had warmed on the stove, then tucked her into bed.

"Sirius?" Maggie asked sleepily.

"Sleeping safely by the stove," Ma answered. "Your dog saved over a hundred people today. You can be right proud of him."

"He's a good boy," said Maggie. The wind still rattled the windows and whistled through the crab apple tree. "Is Pa back yet?"

"Not yet. I'm sure he'll be home tomorrow," her mother answered.

Maggie fell into a deep sleep as the stars and the new moon sparkled over Bonnie Bay.

Sunday morning came bright and fresh. Sirius got up and stretched as Maggie entered the kitchen. On the table was a note.

Maggie,

I've gone to church. There's a special thanksgiving service for the town and the passengers. You were so tired, I didn't want to wake you.

No word yet from Pa and Marcus, but try not to worry. There are very few outports along the way with wireless stations where they could contact us.

Love, Ma

Maggie bowed her head. "Thank you, Lord, for saving everyone last night—including Sirius." Sirius thumped his tail. "And please, *please*, bring Pa home safely so we can all be together and happy again. Amen," she whispered. "Oh, and one more thing," she added. "The Rands know that Sirius is here. Please protect him from that law."

After breakfast, Maggie headed for the door. "Come on, Sirius. The Rands wouldn't *dare* hurt you today. Not with all these people in town who owe their lives to you."

As the two were walking down the path, Vera called out, "May I come, too? Ma says I can take a walk in the sunshine." Maggie's cousin looked thin and pale, but her bright smile had returned and her blond hair had begun to grow back.

"Did you hear what happened yesterday?" Maggie asked.

"Ma told me all about it," Vera answered, catching up to Maggie. "And how Sirius brought the line out to the ship in all those big waves. I wish I could have been there." Vera bent down and hugged Sirius, who licked her face. "You *famous, clever dog!*"

The girls sat together near the docks, with Sirius between them. The harbor glistened like a sapphire. Waves lapped gently against the boats. Out by Killock Rock, the steamer had slipped into the deep water and disappeared.

"Yes, I heard *all* about yesterday," said Vera. "It was right brave of you to bring Sirius down to help."

"All those people . . ."

"I know. You couldn't keep your secret anymore. You had to save the passengers."

Maggie nodded. "Remember the eleven ravens?"

"'*A secret that will never be told,*'" Vera quoted.

"Well, everyone knows now that Sirius is here, so *that* wasn't the secret never to be told after all." Maggie grinned and imitated her father's gruff voice: "That's a lot of superstitious non-sense."

"*Pishogue!*" both girls said together.

Vera giggled. "Maggie, were you asleep when they brought you home yesterday?"

"I remember riding in Otto's wagon, but that's all."

"It wasn't Otto's wagon. It was Howard Rand's wagon. I was watching from the door. It was duck-ish—still sort of light—and I could see Howard Rand carrying you into the house."

"No, not so," Maggie said. "You're playing games with me."

"Sirius was in the wagon, too. Pa said Howard yelled, 'God bless this dog,' over and over."

Was Vera so much her old self that she was full of tricks again? "Stop it, Vera . . ."

"*And* my pa said that Howard cried when Marie and his grandson got to shore. Can you imagine that? Howard Rand cried!"

"Oh, good morrow to you," Maggie sputtered. "I can't believe that."

"It's the truth, I swear."

The two girls listened to the music that was

drifting from the church. Sirius lay down at their feet in the sunlight and closed his eyes. A gull soared overhead.

"I'm glad we didn't have to sit through another one of Reverend Dobbs's boring sermons," Maggie said.

"Aren't they awful? Oh, church is over," said Vera. "People are coming out."

Sirius led the way to the churchyard gate. "Do you see my mother?" Maggie asked, holding her hand over her eyes against the sun to scan the crowd. She gasped. Howard Rand and Joey Harper were standing at the door talking to the Reverend Dobbs.

"Quick, we've got to get away." Maggie grabbed Sirius's collar. But it was too late. The men were coming toward her.

"Maggie Wells," the constable called.

Maggie pulled Sirius. "Run, Sirius," she commanded, but crowds of people were milling around her, blocking the way.

"There's the dog. There's Sirius!" someone called. Now people were gathered all around Maggie, separating her from Vera.

"Please, let us go!" Maggie begged.

Howard Rand clamped his large hand on her shoulder. "Maggie, don't run, maid. We were looking for you at church. This was a special service."

Maggie tried to wriggle away, but Howard held her fast. "The service wasn't right without you there—you and your dog," he said, glancing down at Sirius, who stood alert by Maggie.

"That's right," said Joey Harper. "This dog saved everyone on that ship out there. We wanted you both to be there this morning so we could all thank you."

"What . . . what about the law—the sheepdog law? You were going to shoot Sirius. I saw you with your rifles." Maggie still held on tightly to Sirius's collar.

Joey Harper nodded. "There have been several sheep killed by dogs around here, Maggie."

Howard Rand shook his head. "Tamar was sure it was your dog. She was right upset and cross as the cats when it happened to her own sheep, let me tell."

Maggie looked around for Ma. What was Howard Rand saying? What would they do to

Sirius? She could see Ma pushing through the crowd.

"I'm here, Maggie," Ma said, stepping close to her daughter.

"I was angry at the dogs—and I was angry with your father," Howard Rand continued. "I heard about the new boat and how my best fishermen were going to leave me and go with your pa." He put both hands on Maggie's shoulders. "Will you forgive me, maid? I've been a gommel and a fool. There's enough fish in the sea for all of us. And if your pa doesn't get home by noon, I'm going out to look for him myself." Then he got down on his knees in front of Sirius. "Will you forgive me, Sirius?"

Sirius gave Howard Rand a slobbery kiss on the face.

"I guess that means we've made amends." Howard laughed, wiping his face with his sleeve.

Maggie couldn't believe what she was hearing. "You won't shoot Sirius?"

"No one on the Island of Newfoundland will lay a hand on that dog as long as I'm alive," Howard Rand swore, getting to his feet.

Joyful cheers and applause erupted from the crowd. Maggie was relieved to see Vera's smiling face nearby.

"But what about the law?" Ma asked Joey Harper.

"If your dog is a sheepdog, you all have nothing to fear from the law."

Constance Rand, who had joined her husband, looked around. "Tamar," she called. "Haven't you got something to tell Maggie?"

Tamar stepped forward. She looked at the ground, biting her lip. "Maggie," she said, "as soon as my next lamb is born, it will be yours. I'm giving it to you. That will make you a sheepherder, and it will make Sirius a sheepdog. Then Sirius will be safe forever. I'm sorry I treated you so badly. If you never forgive me, I won't blame you." A little smile played on her lips. "But I hope you will." She looked over at Vera and added, "I hope you *both* will."

Holding her baby, Marie came up to Maggie and kissed her. "There are no words to thank you," she said. "Or you, Sirius." The baby giggled and stretched out his hand toward the dog. "See?" said Marie. "Benjamin wants to thank you, too."

The Reverend Dobbs pushed his way toward the group. "Well, you missed the best sermon I ever gave, Maggie," he said. "It was about self-sacrifice and love of neighbor—"

Howard Rand interrupted with a laugh. "The sermon's over, Pastor, and church is out. Now we're going to have that party. And *everyone* is invited!"

Later, when Vera and most of the islanders had gone home to dinner, Otto and Cliff went onto the wharves to check the storm damage to the smaller boats. Maggie and Ma stayed by the docks, waiting for some word of *The Grace*.

Maggie saw Lucy and Annie standing off by themselves, looking out to sea.

Ma went over and put her arm around Lucy. "They'll be back," she said. "You'll see."

Lucy gave a weak smile and nodded.

Maggie and Sirius joined them.

Annie said, "Maggie, your dog was right brave to go out in those waves and save all the passengers."

"Sirius is the most wonderful dog in all the world," said Maggie.

Sirius barked at a soaring gull. Maggie remembered the eleven ravens she had seen flying over the *quidnunc* and the secret that would never be told.

There were no more secrets now.

Suddenly, a horn blasted from out beyond the bay. A boat as white as a swan appeared around the arm of the harbor. It honked over and over as it chugged into Bonnie Bay.

Maggie could just make out her father's hat and his cream-colored gansey sweater. "It's Pa!" she screamed.

"That's my Marcus waving from the bow," Lucy exclaimed. She and Ma hurried down the steps to the wharf.

Cliff and Otto had already raced to the open berth where *The Grace* would be docked. They jumped up and down, waving at the boat.

Maggie, Annie, and Sirius scrambled down to the dock.

"Pa," Maggie called. Sirius ran in circles, barking and panting.

As the boat puttered into its berth, Marcus threw the bowline to Otto, then hopped off the boat. "What a trip! You'll never believe the stories we've got to tell." He hugged his wife and daughter.

"Are you all right?" Lucy asked.

"All right?" Marcus guffawed loudly. "In all that sea, I never got sick once." He grabbed Annie and swung her around. "In fact, I've never felt better in my life!"

Maggie and Ma threw themselves into Pa's arms. He kissed them on their cheeks.

"Thank the Lord you're back," said Ma, kissing him back. "We were so worried."

"Now we're all safe—even Sirius," Maggie said. "And have *we* got stories to tell *you*!"

Sirius barked and jumped on Pa, whining and licking his face. "Oh, kisses from you, too, you slobbery old dog?" Pa said, laughing.

Shadows flickered over the dock. "Look, Maggie." Pa pointed up to the sky. "Are those five huge crows that I see? A time to *laugh* and skip about." He grabbed Ma's and Maggie's hands and wheeled them around and around. Sirius jumped and barked happily.

In the blue sky over Bonnie Bay, the black birds soared, then settled, one after another, in a tree high on the *quidnunc*.

AFTERWORD

Almost five hundred years before Christopher Columbus discovered America, Vikings had a settlement at L'Anse aux Meadows, on the northern peninsula of Newfoundland. Today, Newfoundland, along with Labrador, is a province of Canada and has half a million inhabitants who affectionately call their island "the Beautiful Rock."

Since childhood I have heard the sayings, songs, and stories of my mother's birthplace—a fishing village called Moreton's Harbor, in Newfoundland. My earliest memory is when I was two years old and visited the island for the very first time. I remember picking partridgeberries with Mother, on top of a cliff, hundreds of feet above Notre Dame Bay.

Star in the Storm is based upon actual events, but the characters and circumstances are fictional. The church, the cliffs, the *quidnunc*, and the icebergs are real. During World War II, a little girl from Moreton's Harbor did row out to an iceberg to bring back fresh ice to my mother's sick younger brother. At that time there was no electricity there and no refrigeration. Iceberg water is clean and pure—and cold! Icebergs break away from the glaciers of Greenland to the north of Newfoundland and are abundant in the waters off the island. The area below the cliffs is sometimes called Iceberg Alley. No one really knows when Newfoundland dogs (or "Newfs") like Sirius were first bred, but some folks say they were originally half mastiff and half Saint Bernard. Most Newfoundlands are black, and some have white markings. Others are gray, brown, or white. Newfoundland breeders take nose-prints of their dogs for identification purposes, since no two Newfs have the same nose-print.

Newfoundlands were originally bred to be working dogs on land and water. Fishing and merchant vessels often kept a Newf on board as part of the crew. Newfs are big, gentle, playful, and make great lifeguards. Their webbed feet act like paddles, and their tails help them to steer, like a rudder on a boat. Their thick fur protects them from cold water temperatures. Newfs swim using the breaststroke instead of a dog paddle, and they can dive into deep water. Today, Newfoundlands are still used as working dogs, but they are bred all over the world and make terrific pets.

Newfoundlands are famous for rescuing children and fishermen. The rescue that Sirius performs is based upon the most well-known rescue performed by a Newf. That was back in the early 1900s, when a dog carried a line for a breeches buoy through treacherous waves to a foundering steamer. That dog saved one hundred people, including a baby that was sent across the water to safety in a mailbag.

The verse about black birds that Maggie quotes throughout the story is one that Mother taught me when I was a child. While black ravens are native to Newfoundland, Mother said the verse was about crows, and most Newfoundlanders feel that the verse is about crows. Whether crows or ravens, whenever a flock of black birds appears, I find myself counting them, just as Maggie does.

The colorful language, superstitions, and folklore

in my story have been collected from all over New-foundland. The pronunciation of certain words and the meanings of some lore vary from one harbor or village to another. I've gathered them together and given them to my characters, who dwell in one imaginary outport—Bonnie Bay.

Someday I hope you will visit Newfoundland and see the towering cliffs, the glistening icebergs, the Newfoundland dogs, and meet the gracious people who call the Beautiful Rock their home.

J. H. H.

Venice, Florida

January 1999

How I came to write
Star in the Storm

"My mother, a Newfoundlander, was a great storyteller. When I was a child, she told me stories about her birthplace in Newfoundland; she reeled off songs of shipwrecks and ghosts that turned my blood to ice! She'd retell folk tales from ancient Scotland, England, and Wales. And she related amazing stories about heroic rescues by Newfoundland dogs. I would listen, totally entranced. 'Is this a true story?' I'd ask her. 'Of course! It has a little bit of *true*; and a little bit of *story*,' she'd answer. My mother knew how to weave true events into fiction—by adding a pinch of imagination, a touch of drama, and lots of love. After all, that's what storytellers do! Many of the incidents that the dog, Sirius, performs in my book, *Star in the Storm*, are based upon true happenings. The Newfoundland dogs my mom knew in the land of her birth, *did* fetch tools from shore to boats—and vice versa. One dog *did* rescue a child stranded in a rowboat. Another dog jumped off a cliff to save a sheep. I used these and other actual events in my story. Although Sirius himself is a fictional dog, he is made up of many wonderful, loving, brave dogs—and he has become real to me. In *Star in the Storm* I've woven a little bit of *true*; and a little bit of *story*, a pinch of imagination, a touch of drama, and lots of love. Well, what do you know? I turned out to be a storyteller, too!"

Joan Hiatt Harlow